GRANNY

Anthony Horowitz

First published in 1994
by Walker Books Ltd
This Large Print edition published by
BBC Audiobooks Ltd
by arrangement with
Walker Books Ltd
2005

ISBN 1 4056 6072 4

British Library Cataloguing in Publication Data

Horowitz, Anthony, 1955–
 Granny.—Large print ed.
 1. Grandmothers—Juvenile fiction 2. Children's stories
 3. Large type books
 I. Title
 823. 9'14[J]

ISBN 1-4056-6072-4

Printed and bound in Great Britain by
Antony Rowe Ltd., Chippenham, Wiltshire

For my sister, Caroline

CONTENTS

PROLOGUE:
HEATHROW AIRPORT

The storm broke early in the evening and by seven o'clock it looked as if Heathrow might have to shut down. Runway One had disappeared in the rain. Runway Two was a canal. Half the planes had been delayed and the other half were circling hopelessly above the clouds, waiting their turn to land. The wind had blown an Air France DC10 all the way to Luton while, in a Jumbo Jet from Tokyo, seventy-nine Japanese passengers had all been sick at the same time. It was a night no one would forget.

The green Mercedes reached the airport at exactly half past seven, skidding round a corner and spraying water over two traffic wardens, a porter and a visitor from Norway. Swerving across the road, it missed a taxi by inches and rocketed into the car park of Terminal Three. The electric side

1

window slid down and a hand with a signet ring and the initials GW entwined in gold reached out to pluck a parking ticket from the machine. Then the car jumped forward again, shot up three ramps with the tyres screaming and crashed into a wall. Ten thousand pounds' worth of metal and paintwork crumpled in on itself. The engine died. Steam hissed from beneath the bent and broken bonnet.

The doors of the car opened and three people got out. The driver was a short, bald man. Next to him was a woman in a fur coat. The back seat had been occupied by a twelve-year-old boy.

'You told me to park on the fourth floor!' the man screamed. 'The fourth floor!'

'Yes, Gordon . . .' the woman muttered.

'But this car park's only got three floors!' the man moaned. He pointed at the wreck of his car. 'And now look what's happened!'

'Oh, Gordon . . .' The woman's lips quivered. For a moment she looked terrified. Then she blinked. 'Does it really matter?' she asked.

The man stared at her. 'You're right!' he exclaimed. He laughed out loud. 'It doesn't matter at all! We're leaving the car here! We'll never see it again . . .!'

The man and the woman rushed into each other's arms, kissed each other and then grabbed their luggage, which the boy had meanwhile taken out of the boot. They had only two suitcases between them and these looked as if they had been packed in a hurry. Part of a pink silk tie, a striped pyjama leg and a frilly shower cap were poking out of one side.

'Come on!' the man exclaimed. 'Let's go . . .'

But just then there was a flash of lightning and an explosion of thunder and the three of them froze, alone in the middle of the dimly lit car park. A plane roared past overhead.

'Oh, Gordon . . .' the woman whimpered.

'It's all right,' Gordon snapped. 'She's not here. Keep your hair on.

We're going to be all right. I'd keep my hair on except I packed it . . .'

'Come on. We've got to get the tickets,' the boy said. And without waiting for his parents he began to walk towards the lifts.

Ten minutes later, the family was queuing up at the British Airways ticket desk. After the darkness of the storm, the building was unnaturally bright, like a television set with the colour turned up too much. There were people everywhere, milling around with their suitcases and carrier bags. A policeman with a machine gun patrolled the area. He was the only person smiling.

'Good evening, sir.' The man at the ticket desk was in his early twenties with close-cropped hair and tired eyes. He had his name—OWEN—on a badge on his chest but in his tiredness he had pinned it on upside down. 'Can I help you?'

'You certainly can, Nemo,' the man said, squinting at the badge. 'I want three flights . . .'

'Three flights, sir?' Owen coughed.

He had never seen such nervous-looking passengers. They all looked as if they had just come off the worst fairground ride in the world. 'Where to?' he asked.

'America,' the man replied.

'Africa,' the woman said at the same moment.

'Australia,' the boy exclaimed. 'Anywhere!' the man said. 'Just so long as it leaves soon.'

'And it's got to be far away!' the woman added.

'Well, sir . . .' Owen swallowed. 'It would help if you actually knew where you wanted to go . . .'

The man leaned forward, his eyes wild and staring. (They weren't staring in quite the same direction, which made him look even more wild.) His clothes were expensive—tailor-made— but the ticket salesman couldn't help noticing that he had dressed in a hurry. His tie was crooked and, more surprisingly, on the wrong side of his neck.

'I just want to go away,' the man hissed, 'before *she* gets here.'

5

The woman burst into tears and tried to hide her face in her mink coat. The boy began to tremble. The ticket-seller's eyes flickered to the computer screen in front of him. The computer screen flickered back. 'How about the nine o'clock flight to Perth?' he suggested.

'Scotland!' The man screamed the word so loudly that several passengers turned to look at him and the policeman dropped his machine gun.

'Australia,' the ticket-seller said.

'Perthect!' the man exclaimed. He snapped a gold Visa card onto the counter. 'We'll have two tickets first class and one in tourist for the boy. Ow!' The man cried out as his wife's elbow caught him on the side of his head. 'All right,' he said, rubbing a red mark above his eye. 'We'll all go first class together.'

'Certainly, sir.' The ticket-seller picked up the credit card. 'Mr Gordon Warden?'

'Yes. That's me.'

'And the child's name?'

'Jordan Warden.'

6

'Jordan Warden.' The ticket-seller tapped the name into the computer. 'And your wife . . . ?'

'Maud N. Warden,' the woman said.

'Gordon Warden. Jordan Warden. Maud N. Warden. Right . . .' He tapped some more buttons and waited as the machine spat out three tickets. 'Check in at Desk 11. And it'll be Gate 6 for boardin' Mr Warden.'

*   *   *

Five hours later, British Airways Flight 777 took off for Perth in Western Australia. As the plane reached the end of the runway and lurched upwards into the swirling night and rain, Gordon Warden and his wife sank back into their first class seats. Mr Warden began to giggle. 'We've done it,' he said in a quivering voice. 'We've beaten her . . .'

'How do you know she's not on the plane?' his wife asked.

Mr Warden sat bolt upright. 'Stewardess!' he called. 'Bring me a parachute!'

Just across the aisle, Jordan strained in the soft half-light to get a sight of the other passengers. Had they really done it? Or were they going to see that terrible, wrinkled face turning slowly to leer at them in the crowded cabin?

The plane reached thirty thousand feet and turned south on the first leg of its journey across the world.

The events that had begun nine months before were finally over.

GRANNY'S FOOTSTEPS

Nine months before, the Wardens had been a wealthy and—to all appearances—happy family living in a large house in North London. The house was called Thattlebee Hall.

It was a huge place with eleven bedrooms, five living-rooms, three staircases and about a mile of thickly-carpeted corridors. You could have played tennis in one of the bathrooms—which was something Mr and Mrs Warden occasionally did, quite naked, using the soap as a ball. It was also very easy to get lost. One man—who had come to read the gas meter—actually stayed there for three days before anyone noticed him, and that was only because he had parked his gas van in the hall.

The family occupied the main body of the house. There was a nanny, Mrs Jinks, with rooms on the top floor. The west wing was occupied by two

Hungarian servants—Wolfgang and Irma. And there was even a smaller house at the bottom of the garden where the gardener, a very old man called Mr Lampy, lived with two cats and a family of moles that he had been too kind-hearted to gas.

Gordon Warden, the head of the family, was a short and rather plump man in his early fifties. He was of course extremely wealthy. 'My suits are tailor-made, my private yacht is sailor-made and I drink champagne like lemonade.' This was something he often liked to say. He smoked cigars that were at least eight inches long even though he could seldom get to the last inch without being sick. His wife, Maud, also smoked—cigarettes in her case. Sometimes, at dinner, there would be so much smoke in the room that they would be unable to see each other and guests would be gasping for fresh air by the time coffee was served.

They also saw very little of their only child. They were not cruel people but the fact was that there was no room for children in their world. To Mr Warden, children meant runny noses, illnesses and noise—which is why he employed a nanny, at great expense, to handle all that for him. Even so, he always made sure he spent at least five minutes with Jordan when he got home in the evening. He nearly always remembered his birthday. And he would smile pleasantly if he happened to pass his son in the street.

Mr Warden was a businessman but he never spoke about his business. This was because it was almost certainly illegal. Nobody knew exactly what he did but some things were certain. If Mr Warden saw a policeman approaching he would dive into the bushes, and he seldom went anywhere without a luxurious false moustache. Mr Warden loved luxury. As well as the made-to-measure suits, he had a liking for silk shirts and shoes made from endangered species. He had a gold tie, a gold signet ring and three gold teeth. He was particularly proud of the teeth and as a special sign of affection had left them to his wife in his will.

Maud Warden did not work. She had

never worked, not even at school, and as a consequence could not read or write. She was however a very fine bridge player. She played bridge twice a week, went out to lunch three times a week, and went riding on the days that were left. To amuse herself, she had piano lessons, tennis lessons and trapeze lessons. Sometimes to please her husband she would play a Chopin nocturne or a Beethoven sonata. But he actually much preferred it when she put on her spangly leotard and swung in the air, suspended from the ceiling by her teeth.

The Wardens had one child and weren't even certain quite how they had ended up with him. Although he had been christened Jordan Morgan Warden, he liked to call himself Joe.

Joe did not like his parents. He didn't like the house, the garden, the cars, the huge meals, the cigarette smoke . . . any of it. It was as if he had been born in a prison cell, a very comfortable one certainly, but a prison nonetheless. All day long he dreamed of escaping. One day he would be a trapeze artist in a circus, the next a flier in the Royal Air Force. He dreamed of running away to Bosnia and becoming a relief worker or hiking to the very north of Scotland and looking after sheep. He wanted to be hungry, to feel cold, to have adventures and to know danger and he was angry because he knew that so long as he was a child none of this would be his.

The strange truth is that many rich children have a much worse life and are much less happy than poor children. This was certainly the case for Joe.

To look at, he was a rather short boy with dark hair and a round face. He had brown eyes but when he was day-dreaming they would soften and turn almost blue. Joe had very few friends, and what friends he did have were unfortunately just like him, locked up in their own homes and gardens. The two people closest to him were Mrs Jinks, his nanny, and Mr Lampy, the gardener. Often he would go down to the bottom of the garden and sit in the old shed with the two cats and the family of moles and the strange smell of gin that always hovered in the air.

'Next week I'm going,' he would say. 'I'm really going. I'm going to join the Foreign Legion. Do you think they take twelve-year-olds?'

'I wouldn't join the Foreign Legion, Master Warden,' the gardener would reply. 'Too many foreigners for me.'

'Don't call me "Master Warden"! My name is Joe.'

'That's right, Master Warden. That's what it is.'

This, then, was life at Thattlebee Hall. But there was one other member of the family. She didn't live with the Wardens but she was somehow never far away. And the whole family, everything, would change with her coming. Even the sound of her footsteps approaching the front door would be enough to trigger it off. *Scrunch . . . scrunch . . . scrunch.* Suddenly the sun would seem to have gone in and the shadows would stretch out like a carpet unrolling to welcome the new arrival.

Granny.

She always came to the house by taxi and she never gave the driver a tip. She was a short woman and every year she seemed a little shorter. She had wiry silver hair which looked all right from a distance—only when you got closer could you see right through to the speckled pink surface of her skull. Her clothes, even on the hottest summer day, were thick and heavy, as were her spectacles. These were enormous with bright gold frames and two different sorts of glass. Once, just for a joke, Joe tried them on. He was still bumping into things two weeks later.

Her real name was Ivy Kettle (she was Mrs Warden's mother) but nobody had called her that since she had turned seventy. From that time on she had simply been Granny. Not Grandma. Not Grandmother. Just Granny. Somehow it suited her.

There was a time when Joe had liked his granny and had looked forward to her visits. She seemed to take a real interest in him—more so than his own parents—and she was always winking and smiling at him. Often she would give him sweets or fifty pence pieces. But as he grew older, he had begun to notice things about his granny that he had not noticed before.

First there were the physical details: the terrible caves in her wrists where the skin seemed to sag underneath the veins, the blotchy patches on her legs, the whiskers on her upper lip and the really quite enormous mole on her chin. She had no dress sense whatsoever. She had, for example, worn the same coat for *twenty-seven years* and it had probably been second-hand when she bought it. Granny was very mean to everyone. But she was meanest to herself. She never bought any new clothes. She never went to the cinema. She said she would prefer to wait and see the films on video even though she was far too mean to buy a machine to play them on. She had a pet cat which she never fed. Tiddles was so thin that one day it was attacked by a budgerigar and that was the last time it was ever seen. As for the money and sweets that she gave Joe, Mrs Warden had actually slipped them to her when

16

she arrived. It was simply an arrangement to make Joe like Granny more.

Then there were her table manners. Although it's a sad thing to say, Granny's table manners would have made a cannibal sick. She had a large mouth framed by some of the yellowest teeth in the world. These teeth were stumpy and irregular, slanting at odd angles, and actually wobbled in her gums when she laughed. But how hard they worked! Granny would eat at a fantastic rate, shovelling food in with a fork, lubricating it with a quick slurp of water and then swallowing it with a little sucking noise and a final hiccup. Sitting at the table, she would remind you of a cement mixer at a building site and watching her eat was both fascinating and repulsive at the same time.

Another aspect of her bad table manners was her tendency to steal the silver. After lunch with Granny, Mr Warden would insist on a spoon count. Wolfgang and Irma would spend hours in the pantry checking off the pieces that remained against the pieces that had been laid and then writing down a long list of what would have to be replaced. When Granny left the house at half past four or whenever, her twenty-seven-year-old coat would be a lot bulgier than when she arrived, and as she leaned over to kiss Joe goodbye, he would hear the clinking in her pockets. On one occasion, Mrs Warden embraced her mother too enthusiastically and actually impaled herself on a fruit knife. After that, Mr Warden installed a metal detector in the front door which did at least help.

But nobody in the family ever mentioned this—either to each other or to anyone else. Mr Warden was never rude to his mother-in-law. Mrs Warden was always pleased to see her. Nobody acted as if anything was wrong.

Joe became more and more puzzled about this—and more confused about his own feelings. He supposed he loved her. Didn't all children love their grandparents? But *why* did he love her? One day he tackled Mrs Jinks on the subject.

'Do you like Granny, Mrs Jinks?' he asked.

'Of course I do,' his nanny replied.

'But why? She's got wrinkled skin. Her teeth are horrible. And she steals the knives and forks.'

Mrs Jinks frowned at him. 'That's not her fault,' she said. 'She's old . . .'

'Yes. But . . .'

'There is no but.' Mrs Jinks gave him the sort of look that meant either a spoonful of cod-liver oil or a hot bath. 'Always remember this, Joe,' she went on. 'Old people are special. You have to treat them with respect and never make fun of them. Just remember! One day you'll be old too . . .'

LOVE FROM GRANNY

If Joe had doubts about Granny, the Christmas of his twelfth year was when they became horrible certainties.

Christmas was always a special time at Thattlebee Hall: specially unpleasant, unfortunately. For this was when the whole family came together and Joe found himself surrounded by aunts and uncles, first cousins and second cousins—none of whom he particularly liked. And it wasn't just him. None of them liked each other either and they always spent the whole day arguing and scoring points off each other. One Christmas they had actually had a fight in the course of which Aunty Nita had broken Uncle David's nose. Since then, all the relations came prepared and as they trooped into the house, the metal detector would bleep like crazy, picking up the knives, crowbars and knuckle-dusters that they had concealed in their clothes.

Joe had four cousins who were only a few years older than him but who never spoke to him. They were very fat, with ginger hair and freckles and pink legs that oozed out of tight, short trousers, like sausages out of a sausage machine. They were terribly spoiled of course, and always very rude to Joe. This was one of the reasons he didn't like them. But the main one was that Joe realized that if his parents had their way, he would end up just like them. They were reflections of him in a nightmare, distorted mirror.

But the star of Christmas Day was Granny. She was the head of the family and always came a day early, on Christmas Eve, to spend the night in the house. Joe would watch as the house was prepared for her coming.

First the central heating would be turned up. It would be turned up so high that by eleven o'clock all the plants had died and the windows were so steamed up that the outside world had disappeared. Then her favourite chair would be moved into her favourite place with three cushions—

one for her back, one for her neck and one for her legs. A silver dish of chocolates would be placed on a table, carefully selected so only the soft centres remained. And a large photograph of her in a gold frame would be taken out of the cupboard under the stairs and placed in the middle of the mantelpiece.

This had been happening every year for twelve years. But this year Joe noticed other things too. And he was puzzled.

First of all, Irma and Wolfgang were both in a bad mood. At breakfast, Irma burned the toast whilst Wolfgang spent the whole morning sulking, muttering to himself in Hungarian, which is a sulky enough language at the best of times. His parents were irritable too. Mrs Warden bit her nails. Mr Warden bit Mrs Warden. By midday they had consumed an entire bottle of whisky between them, including the glass.

Joe had seen this sort of behaviour before. It was always the same when Granny came to visit. But it was only now that he began to wonder. Were they like this *because* Granny was coming? Could it be that they didn't actually want to see her at all?

It was seven o'clock on the evening of Christmas Eve when Granny finally arrived. She had told Mr Warden that she would be coming at lunch and Wolfgang had been dutifully waiting at the door since then. When the taxi did finally draw up, the unfortunate man was so covered in snow that only his head was showing and he was too cold to announce she was there. It was a bad start.

'I've been waiting out here for ten minutes,' Granny muttered as Mrs Warden opened the door after just two. 'Really, dear. You know this weather doesn't agree with me. I'm going to have to go to bed straight away—although goodness knows I won't sleep. This house is far too cold.'

'What are you thinking of, Wolfgang?' Mrs Warden sighed, gazing at the blue nose and forehead which was just about all she could see of her faithful Hungarian servant.

Granny stepped into the house,

23

leaving her luggage on the drive where the taxi driver had dumped it.

'A little brandy?' Mrs Warden suggested.

'A large one.'

Granny stood in the hall waiting for someone to help her off with her coat and at the same time examining her surroundings with a critical eye. Mr Warden had recently bought a new Picasso of which he was very proud. It hung by the door and she noticed it now. 'I don't think very much of that, dear. Too many squiggles and it doesn't go with the wallpaper.'

'But Mummy, it's a Picasso!'

'A piano? Don't be ridiculous. It doesn't look anything like a piano.' Granny could be deaf when she wanted to be. At other times she could hear a pin drop half a mile away. She moved towards the living-room then suddenly stopped and pointed. 'But I like that very much,' she said. 'How original! And what a lovely colour!'

'But Mummy. That's not a painting. That's a damp patch.'

Joe had watched all this from the

first floor landing but hearing Mrs Jinks opening a door behind him, he realized he had to show him-self. Quickly he stood up and went down the stairs.

'Hello, James!' Granny cooed. 'You've put on a lot of weight!'

'My name's Joe, not James,' Joe said. He was sensitive about his name. And his weight.

'No, it's not. It's Jordan,' his mother said. 'Really Jordan! Joe is so common!'

'Jordan? That's what I said,' Granny interjected. 'Haven't you grown, Jordan! What a big boy you are! What a big boy!' And with these words, Granny went into a 'spread'.

Joe shuddered. The spread was the word he used to describe what Granny was doing now. It was the one thing he dreaded most.

The spread was the position Granny took when she wanted to be kissed. She widened her legs and crouched down slightly with her arms open as if she wanted him to jump onto her knees and maybe even onto her shoulders. Of course, if Joe had done this, Granny would have broken into several pieces as she was over ninety years old and very frail. And with the spread came the terrible words . . . 'Aren't you going to give your grandma a kiss, then?'

Joe swallowed hard. He was aware that his mother was watching him and that he had to be careful what he did. But at the same time he hated what he knew he had to do.

Kissing Granny was not a pleasant experience. First there was the smell. Like many old ladies, she wore an expensive perfume that was very sweet and very musty and, if you got too close to it, made you feel a little sick. There were no labels on her perfume bottles but this one might have been called 'Decomposing Sheep'. Then there was her make-up. Granny wore a lot of make-up. Sometimes she put it on so thickly that you could have drawn a picture in it with your thumb-nail. Her lipstick was the worst bit. It was bright blood red and no matter how carefully Joe tried, he always came away with a glowing mirror-image of Granny's lips on his cheek. Nobody knew what make of lipstick Granny used, but Mrs Jinks could only get it off him with a Brillo pad.

But worst of all was her skin. As well as kissing her grandson, Granny insisted on his kissing her and her skin was as withery as a punctured balloon. No words could describe the feel of her skin against his lips, actually flapping slightly between the upper and the lower lip at the moment of kissing. One night Joe had woken up screaming. He had just had a nightmare in which he had kissed Granny too enthusiastically and had actually swallowed her whole.

Smack! Granny kissed Joe.

Smeruberry smack! Joe kissed Granny.

Then, with a satisfied smile, she continued into the living-room. Outside, Irma was pouring hot water over Wolfgang to thaw him so that he could carry in the cases. Mr Warden was nowhere to be seen. This was something else that had puzzled Joe— how his father was never around when Granny arrived. The year before, Joe had found him hiding inside the grand piano and he was there now. He could tell from the cigar smoke coming out of the keyboard.

Granny sat down in the chair that had been chosen for her. It was one of those old-fashioned wing chairs and she always sat in it even though her legs couldn't touch the ground, with the result that you could see straight up her dress. Not that you would look. Your eyes would stray up to her bulging knees wrapped in what looked like surgical stockings, and then beyond to the yellowing flesh of her thighs. And that would be enough. Her legs were like a set out of *Dr Who*.

Mrs Warden had poured a large brandy. Granny swallowed it in a single gulp. 'Where's Gordon?' she asked, glancing suspiciously at the piano.

'I don't know . . .' Mrs Warden faltered.

'I can see him, Maud darling. I'm not blind you know . . .'

Mr Warden came out of the piano, hitting his head on the lid with an echoing thud. 'I was tuning it,' he

28

explained.

'I'll have another brandy please, dear. And do you have anything other than this cooking brandy?'

'Cooking brandy?' Mr Warden exploded. 'That's Remy Martin. From Harrods.'

'And I'm sure the Arabs love it,' Granny replied, either mishearing him or pretending to. 'But it burns my throat.'

Nobody slept well that night. The trouble was, Granny was a terrible snorer. At dinner she had complained of a touch of indigestion and an upset stomach after having been kept waiting in the cold and so she was only able to manage three portions of lamb stew, two portions of lemon mousse and half a bottle of wine. Finally she had tottered off to bed and ten minutes later her snores were resounding through the house. Even in the vast surroundings of Thattlebee Hall there was no escaping it. Joe went to sleep with his head buried under five pillows. Mrs Warden finally managed to drop off after squeezing a wax candle into each ear. Mr Warden didn't sleep at all. In the morning there were huge bags under his eyes—and even huger ones on the bedroom floor, which he was busily packing. It took Mrs Warden half an hour and a fountain of tears to persuade him not to move into a hotel.

But it was Christmas Day: the snow sparkled in the garden and the church bells rang. Santa Claus had visited, the smell of turkey wafted through the house and everyone was in a good mood. Even the arrival of all the relations and the terrible crash as Uncle Michael's Volvo accidentally reversed into Uncle Kurt's Rover couldn't completely spoil the scene. The Wardens always waited for everyone to arrive before they opened their presents. Now the whole family repaired to the Christmas tree. Wolfgang, Irma and Mrs Jinks came in to join them and Mr Warden served champagne and orange juice—champagne for his wife and himself, orange juice for everyone else. It was a happy moment. Even Granny was smiling as she tottered out of the breakfast room and took her place in her favourite chair.

Joe found himself sitting between his Uncle David and one of his cousins. There were about fifteen people in the room but as he looked around, he found himself concentrating only on Granny. She was sitting in her usual place, smiling, her legs dangling a few inches above the carpet. Joe gazed at her. Was he imagining it, or was there something strange about Granny's smile? It was as if she were enjoying some secret joke. He had thought at first that she was looking out of the window but now he realized that her eyes were fixed on him. Occasionally her lips quivered and as the presents were handed out she couldn't hold back a soft and high-pitched giggle.

'This is for you, Jordan.'

His father had handed him a present from under the tree. Joe flipped open the label on the top and immediately recognized the large, spidery handwriting.

TO JORDAN. LOVE FROM GRANNY.

Now although there were many presents for Joe under the tree, this was one he was particularly looking forward to and, holding it in his hands, he suddenly felt ashamed. A moment ago he had been looking at his granny as if she were . . . what? Some sort of monster! But he couldn't have been more wrong. She was just a kind old lady, surrounded by her family, enjoying the day. And she loved him. The proof of it was in his hands.

Joe loved science fiction. He had seen *Star Wars* three times and had dozens of books about aliens and space travel on his bedroom shelves. But what he liked best of all was robots— and when Granny had asked him what he wanted for Christmas that was what he had said. He had actually seen one in Hamley's—about half a metre high and packed with all the latest Japanese micro-circuitry. You had to assemble it yourself—and that was the challenge— but when it was finished it would walk, talk, lift and carry . . . all by radio-control.

And there it was now in front of him.

Joe recognized Granny's gift-wrap at once. It was actually wedding paper— she was always economizing like that. It was a large, rectangular box, just the size it should have been. As his fingers tore through the paper he could feel the cardboard underneath. Then the paper was off. The box was open. And his heart and stomach shrank.

The robot was the sort of thing you might give to a two-year-old. It was made of brightly coloured plastic with a stupid, painted face and the name, HANK, written in large letters on its chest. Radio control? It had a key sticking out of its back. Wind it up and it would stagger a few inches across the carpet and fall over, whirring and kicking its legs uselessly. Suddenly Joe realized that everyone was looking at him: his aunts and uncles, Wolfgang, Irma, Mrs Jinks. His four cousins were nudging each other and sniggering. They were all thinking the same thing.

A baby toy! What a baby!

'Do you like it, dear?'

He heard his granny's voice and looked up. And that was when he finally knew. There was something in her face that he had never seen before and now that he had noticed it he would never be able to see her any other way again. It was like one of those optical illusions you sometimes find in cereal packets. You look at a picture one way but then you suddenly notice something different and you can never see it again the same way.

He was right.

She had done it on purpose.

She knew exactly what he wanted and she had gone out and deliberately chosen this baby toy to humiliate him in front of the entire family. Of course, his mother would try to explain that Granny meant well and that she hadn't understood what he wanted. He would be made to write a thank you letter and every lying word would hurt him. But at that moment, looking at her, he knew the truth. He could see it in the wicked glimmer in her eyes, in the half-turned corner of her mouth. And it was so strong, so horrible that he shivered.

She was *evil*. For reasons that he did not yet understand, Granny hated him and wanted to hurt him in any way she could.

Joe shivered.

He knew the truth about Granny even if nobody else in the room could see it. But that wasn't what frightened him.

What frightened him was that Granny knew he knew. And she didn't care.

Maybe she knew that whatever Joe said, nobody would believe him. Or maybe it was something worse. Watching her, hunched up in the middle of the Christmas gauze and glitter, her eyes sliding slowly from left to right, he realized she was planning something. And that something included him.

TEA WITH GRANNY

A few weeks later, Granny invited Joe to tea. She always used to do this towards the end of the holidays but curiously neither Mr nor Mrs Warden were ever available. Mr Warden was at work. And Mrs Warden—who was now having lessons in Chinese cookery—was at wok. And so Mrs Jinks was the only one left to take him.

Up until now, Joe would have quite looked forward to seeing his Granny. But not any more. He knew now, and even the thought of her filled him with dread.

'I don't want to go,' he told Mrs Jinks as she got into the car.

'Why ever not, Jordan? You know how your granny looks forward to seeing you.'

Yes. Like a fox looks forward to seeing chickens, Joe thought. 'I don't like her,' he said.

'That's a cruel thing to say.'

'I think *she's* cruel . . .'

'Now that's quite enough of that!' Mrs Jinks sniffed. 'I suppose you're still thinking about that silly Christmas present. It was a misunderstanding, that's all.'

Joe had set fire to the misunderstanding. He had taken the toy robot to the bottom of the garden and poured lighter fuel over it and then put a match to it. He and old Mr Lampy had watched as it melted, the plastic bubbling and blistering and the colours running into each other so that for a moment it did look like some alien creature before it shrivelled into a black and sticky puddle.

The old gardener had shaken his head. 'You shouldn't ought to have done that, Master Warden.'

'Why not?'

'It should've gone to a charity shop or a hospital. I'm sure there was someone somewhere who'd have wanted it.'

And Joe had felt a twinge of guilt. But it was too late. The robot was gone.

Granny lived in a flat in a tall, modern block called Wisteria Lodge. This was what the estate agents would have called a purpose-built block, although they might not be able to say what its purpose actually was. Perhaps it was simply to house grannies, as hardly anyone in the building was under seventy years of age. Everything in Wisteria Lodge happened in slow motion. The lift had been specially adapted to go so slowly that you couldn't feel it moving. On one occasion it broke down and Mr and Mrs Warden stood in it for three-quarters of an hour before they realized what had happened.

Granny's flat was on the sixth floor with views over a small field and the traffic on the North Circular Road. Once she had lived in a comfortable house in a tree-lined avenue but when that had got too much for her to handle, her daughter had moved her here. It was actually a very pleasant flat

38

with silk curtains, thick carpets, antique furniture and chandeliers but if you asked her about it Granny would shrug and sigh, 'Well, I have to put up with it. I don't have any choice, do I? Oh dear, oh dear. I don't know . . .' And she would look so sorry for herself that you would forget that there were thousands of old people in far smaller places with no heating and no real comfort who would have given their right arm to live here.

'Hello, Jack. How lovely to see you! Come in. Make yourselves comfortable!'

Waves of pure heat shimmered in the air as Jordan stepped unwillingly into the flat, Mrs Jinks gently pushing him from behind. The central heating was on full all the time. Granny had once been given a six-inch cactus by Mr Warden after a business trip to the Sahara and obviously the intense heat suited it for it was now over eleven feet high, dominating the room with brilliant flowers and vicious spikes.

'Come in, Mrs Jinks. What an unusual hat!'

39

'I'm not wearing a hat, Mrs Kettle.'

'Then if I were you, I'd change my hairdresser.'

Granny moved forward and stooped over Jordan. 'So how are you, my dear?' She reached out with a gnarled finger and prodded his cheek. 'Healthy skin. Healthy colour. Full of vitamins?' She winked at Mrs Jinks.

'He gets plenty of vitamins,' Mrs Jinks replied. Granny's comment about the hat had annoyed her, Joe could see.

'And how are his enzymes?' Granny asked.

'His what?' Mrs Jinks enquired.

'His enzymes! Has he got healthy enzymes? What about his cytoplasm?'

Mrs Jinks shook her head. 'I'm sorry, Mrs Kettle,' she said. 'I don't know what you're talking about.'

'Oh, come in!' Granny snarled briefly and jerked a finger into the room.

The table had already been laid for tea and Joe sat down with Mrs Jinks next to him. Briefly, he scanned the food that lay before him. There it was, the same as always. It was incredible,

40

How could a tea possibly be so vile?

First, there were egg mayonnaise sandwiches, but the eggs had been left out so long that the yellows had taken on a greenish tint and they had so much salt in them that they made your eyes water. Then there was herring on a plate—raw and slippery and soused in some sort of particularly sharp vinegar. Granny's home-made cakes were dry and heavy, guaranteed to glue the top of your mouth to the bottom of your mouth with little taste in between. Even the biscuits were horrible: round, colourless things with neither chocolate nor cream but decorated with almond flakes and bits of dessicated cherry that got caught in your teeth.

But by far the worst item on the table was Granny's cream cheese special. Joe caught sight of it and felt his mouth water unpleasantly and his stomach shrivel as if trying to find somewhere to hide. Granny's cream cheese special consisted of just one thing: cream cheese. That was all it was: a big bowl of cream cheese—and he knew that he would be expected to eat it all.

And he couldn't refuse it—that was the worst of it. It was part of his upbringing. Mr Warden insisted that children shouldn't be allowed to leave the table until they had finished everything they had been given. After all, food cost money and the money was his. As a child, Mr Warden had once remained at the table for an astonishing forty-six hours before he had finally given in and agreed to eat a plate of bread-and-butter pudding that his father had given him. The fact of the matter is that the worst thing about parents is often their parents. That's certainly where they get their most rotten ideas.

'I'll just get some serviettes . . .'

Granny hobbled off into the kitchen and Joe quickly turned to Mrs Jinks.

'I can't eat this,' he said.

'Of course you can,' Mrs Jinks replied. But she didn't sound convinced.

'No! Can't you see? She's done it on purpose. She's chosen all the things I can't stand and she's put them here because she knows you'll make me eat them. She's torturing me!'

'Joe—you're going to get a big smack if you go on like this.'

'Why won't you believe me?' The whole conversation had taken place in whispers but these last words rasped in his throat. 'She hates me!'

'She loves you. She's your granny!'

Then Granny returned from the kitchen carrying some faded paper serviettes. 'Not started yet?' she croaked, grinning at Joe.

She put the serviettes down and picked up a green porcelain bowl, filled to the brim with thick cream cheese. Then she forked out a raw herring and laid it on the top. 'That'll give it extra taste,' she cackled. Finally she slid the whole thing towards him and as she did so Joe saw the trembling half-smile on her lips, the rattlesnake eyes that pinned him to his seat. Her long, knobbly fingers with their uneven, yellow nails were scratching at the tablecloth with sheer excitement. Her whole body was coiled up like a spring.

'Now, eat it all up, dear!'

Joe looked at Mrs Jinks but she

turned away as if unwilling to meet his eyes. He looked at the cream cheese, slooping about in the bowl with the herring lying there like a dead slug. Suddenly his mind was made up.

He pushed the bowl away.

'No, thank you,' he said. 'I'm not hungry.'

'What?' Granny gurgled. She had been taken off guard and jerked in her seat as if she had just sat on a drawing pin. 'But . . .' Her mouth opened and shut. 'What's the matter . . .? Mrs Jinks . . .!'

This was what Joe had been most afraid of. Whose side would Mrs Jinks take? And Mrs Jinks herself seemed unsure.

'Aren't you hungry?' she asked.

'No,' Joe said.

'Can't you manage a little bit?'

'I'm not feeling well.'

'Well, in that case . . .' Mrs Jinks turned apologetically to Granny. 'If he's not well . . .' she began.

Granny's face shimmered. It was like looking at a reflection in the sea. One moment there was a look of absolute rage and hatred, the sort of look soldiers must have seen before they were bayoneted by the enemy. But then, with a huge effort, Granny managed to wipe it away, replacing it with a look of hurtful sadness. Huge crocodile tears welled up in her eyes. Her lips drew back and puckered like a healing wound.

'But darling,' she said. 'I spent the whole morning getting it ready. It's your favourite.'

'No, it's not,' Joe said. 'I don't like it.'

'But you've always liked it! Have you been eating chocolate and crisps? Have you spoiled your appetite? Is that it? Mrs Jinks . . .'

What was happening at the table was completely unheard of. It was like that moment in *Oliver Twist* when Oliver asks for more—only in reverse as Joe was asking for less. And normally all hell would have broken loose. But Mrs Jinks had seen the look on Granny's face, the full force of her hatred. Like Joe, she had glimpsed behind the mask—and now she was taking

Joe's side.

'Joe's not hungry,' she said.

'Have a drink!' Granny trilled. 'I've got some hot Ribena in the kitchen.'

'No, thank you.' Joe only liked Ribena cold. For some reason, once it was heated up it went all sweet and sticky.

'How about a nice lemon and honey milk-shake?'

'No,' Joe insisted.

'I could sprinkle some nutmeg on the top!'

'No, thank you.'

'I think I'll take Joe home,' Mrs Jinks said. She wasn't as clever as Granny at hiding her emotions. It was obvious that she wanted to get away.

Granny saw it too. Slowly the anger crept back into her cheeks. Her little eyes widened and there was a soft yellow glow in what should have been their whites. 'This is your fault, Mrs Jinks,' she hissed.

'Mine?' Mrs Jinks was indignant.

'You're not bringing the boy up properly. Filling him up with sweets and biscuits . . .'

'I did no such thing, Mrs Kettle.'

'Then why won't he eat? Why won't he eat?' Granny gesticulated with a trembling fist. The edge of her wrist caught one of the bowls of cream cheese and it flew off the table, landing with a loud plop in her lap. 'Now look what you've made me do!' She got up and took two steps back from the table. It was a mistake. She had forgotten the cactus. 'Aaaagh!' Granny leapt three feet in the air as she came into contact with the spikes, then collapsed in a heap on the floor. Her dress was covered in cream cheese. Her face was quite purple with anger.

Joe had never seen anything like it. It was wonderful and terrifying at the same time. What was Granny going to do? Was she going to mutter the magic words that would turn Mrs Jinks into a spotted toad? Or—more likely—was she merely going to succumb to a massive heart attack?

In the end, she did neither. She got to her feet, took a deep breath and shrivelled back into an old, defeated woman.

'All right,' she muttered with a sigh. 'Take him home. Leave me here on my own. I don't mind. I'll just sit by myself and maybe do some knitting.'

Granny had never knitted anything in her life. Except, maybe, her brow.

And so they left. Mrs Jinks hurried Joe out of the flat and into the lift— although of course that meant the two of them had to spend another ten minutes standing in awkward silence before they reached the ground. Mrs Jinks was flushed and looked worried. And she had every reason to be.

After they had gone, Granny went to the drinks cabinet and grabbed a bottle of brandy. She pulled the cork out with her teeth (although she very nearly pulled her teeth out with the cork) and took a large swig. Then, feeling better, she went over to the telephone and dialled a number. The phone rang many times before it was answered.

'Hello?' came a thin, quavering voice from the other end.

'Is that Mrs Bucket?'

'Yes. This is Elsie Bucket.'

'This is Ivy Kettle speaking.'

'Yes, Ivy, dear. How very nice to hear from you.' But the voice at the other end sounded faintly bored.

'Listen!' Granny spat the word into the receiver. 'I've just had the boy here in my flat. My grandson . . .'

'Jeremy?' now the voice was a little more interested.

'His name's John! Now listen, Mrs Bucket. I've been thinking about Bideford and I've decided. I'm going to bring him along. For you . . .'

'How delightful of you, my dear Ivy.' The voice dripped with icy charm.

'There is just one problem . . .' Granny went on.

'What problem, Ivy?'

'He's got a nanny. A wretched spiteful nanny. I think she may get in our way.'

'Then you'll have to deal with her, my dear. Or do you need help?"I don't need help, thank you, Mrs Bucket!' Granny scowled and chewed air. A lump of cream cheese slithered off her dress and dripped onto her shoes. 'I'll deal with Mrs Jinks,' she said at last. 'And then the boy will be yours . . .'

49

GRANNY vs NANNY

Mrs Jinks liked to say that she belonged to 'the old school' which was strange because she had never actually been to school in her life. She had been Joe's nanny for five years—but the truth is that she would never have taken the job in the first place if it hadn't been for a mistake.

Before she had come to Thattlebee Hall, Mrs Jinks had earned her living by dancing. A plump, blonde-haired woman with shapely legs, she worked at a Soho club where she performed exotic dances with a snake called Anna. The owner of the club had a stutter and introducing the snake—'Anna, an anaconda'—sometimes took him three-quarters of an hour. For this reason Mrs Jinks decided to get a new job and this was when the mistake was made.

She applied to be a dancer at another club, The Blue Balloon in Battersea, but in her haste she dialled the wrong number and got through to

Mrs Warden. Now, as it happened, Mrs Warden had placed an advertisement in the newspaper that very day. Her current nanny, Miss Barking, had just handed in her notice in order to go and fight in the Gulf War and she herself was about to go on holiday. So she needed somebody fast.

Ten minutes later Mrs Warden had hired Mrs Jinks in the belief that she was a nanny and Mrs Jinks had taken the job in the belief that it was as a dancer. By the time the two of them had realized the mistake it was too late. Mr and Mrs Warden had left for a four-week safari in South Africa. And Mrs Jinks was on her own at home with Joe.

For his part, Joe was quite delighted by the error. Aged seven at the time, he had endured six and a half years of Miss Barking—a woman so tough and so muscular that he had often wondered if she was really a woman at all. There was something very attractive about Mrs Jinks. Maybe it was her round, cheerful face, her loud laugh and her generally unsuitable appearance. Maybe it was her pet snake. But she was unquestionably different.

So in the next four weeks Joe taught her everything he knew about nannying—and the fact is that at the end of the day children know more about nannying than nannies themselves. He took her to the library and together they browsed through books such as *Childcare Made Easy* and *Tips for Top Nannies.* He took her through such activities as bathing, dressing and tidying. He even showed her how to tell him off.

The result was that when Mr and Mrs Warden returned from their safari, they found the house more organized and tidier and Joe cleaner and quieter than ever before and the two of them decided to forget how entirely unsuitable the new nanny was.

As for Mrs Jinks, she had soon decided that life as a nanny was much more pleasant than life as an exotic dancer. She smartened her appearance and became a little more severe and soon it was impossible to tell that it was not she who had taught Joe but Joe who had instructed her.

When she had been with the family for one year, Mrs Jinks took a two-week holiday in the Amazon basin where, one evening, she quietly returned her anaconda to the wild. She never spoke about the snake again. But she always kept a photograph of it in a frame beside her bed.

*　　　*　　　*

Joe only ever mentioned the tea with Granny once—and that was the following day.

'What's an enzyme?' he asked Mrs Jinks, remembering the word Granny had used.

'I don't know,' Mrs Jinks replied, a frown on her face. She sighed. 'We'd better look it up.'

And so they did. They went to the library and looked up the word in a medical dictionary and this is what it said:

Enzymes. The organic substances which accelerate chemical processes occurring in living organisms. Enzyme mechanisms are the key to all biological processes.

'What does that all mean?' Joe asked.

Mrs Jinks slammed the book. 'It doesn't matter,' she said. 'I don't think your granny knew what she was talking about. We won't mention it again.'

But Mrs Jinks was never quite the same after this particular encounter with Granny. There was a worried look in her eyes. Loud noises—a slamming door or a car backfiring—jolted her. Joe got the impression that she was walking a tightrope and was afraid of falling off at any time.

And then the thefts began.

It was the second week in February and Granny had come for lunch. Joe hadn't seen her since the tea and he had been dreading it, but in fact she couldn't have been more pleasant. She gave him a smaller-than-usual kiss and a larger-than-usual present of one pound which hadn't even been given to her by her daughter in the usual way. She ate her lunch without complaining, complimented Irma (who immediately dropped all the dishes) and left all the knives and forks on the table.

It was only as she was leaving, as Wolfgang handed her her twenty-seven-year-old coat, that she let out a sudden scream.

'My cameo brooch!' she exclaimed. Tears welled in her eyes. 'My beautiful cameo brooch. It's gone!'

'Are you sure you were wearing it, Mummy?' Mrs Warden asked.

'Of course I'm sure. I put it on specially. It was on the lapel of my coat.'

'Well, maybe it's dropped off.'

'No, no,' Granny wailed. 'I pinned it quite securely.' She turned to Mrs Jinks. 'You didn't happen to see it, did you, Mrs Jinks?' she asked with a quizzical smile.

'No, Mrs Kettle,' the nanny replied. Two pin-pricks of pink had appeared in her cheeks. 'Why should *I* have seen it?'

'Well . . .' Granny couldn't have looked more innocent. 'You have often admired my cameo brooch. And I did see you looking in the hall cupboard just before lunch.'

'Are you suggesting . . . ?' Mrs Jinks didn't know what to say. Her cheeks were now dark red with anger.

'I wasn't suggesting anything,' Granny interrupted. She almost sang the words and her whole body was shaking with pleasure.

Once again her lips slid away from her teeth in a yellowy smile. 'I'm sure Wolfgang will find it in the garden.'

But Wolfgang never did find the brooch and the next time Granny came for lunch, the whites of her eyes were quite red from weeping. In fact she was crying so much that instead of her usual tiny lace handkerchief she had brought along a tea towel.

'Never mind, Mumsy,' Mrs Warden said. 'I'll buy you another one. Don't be so upset. It's only a piece of jewellery.'

That was the day that Mrs Warden found her diamond earrings had gone missing. She screamed the house down.

'My earrings, Gordon!' she screeched. 'My lovely earrings. They matched my ears! How can they have gone? Oh no . . . !'

'Someone get her a tea towel,' Mr Warden muttered. He was trying to read the *Financial Times.* 'And put it in her mouth.'

'Were they your diamond earrings, darling?' Granny asked. She was sitting in her usual chair, her face a picture of innocence.

'Yes,' Mrs Warden sobbed.

'How sad. You know, Mrs Jinks was saying to me only the other day how much she liked those earrings. What a shame that they've suddenly disappeared . . .'

Joe was as puzzled as anyone by the thefts but already a nasty thought was forming in his mind. Two thefts. Both had taken place on days when Granny was in the house. And twice Granny had pointed the finger at Mrs Jinks . . .

That night, Joe got out of bed and crept downstairs. The hall was dark but he could see light spilling out underneath the door of the living-room. He pressed his ear against the wood. As he had thought, his parents were inside.

'Someone must have taken them,' Mrs Warden was saying. 'They can't have just walked out of the drawer.'

'But who?' That was Mr Warden's voice.

'Well, Mummy was saying that Mrs Jinks . . .'

'Mrs Jinks would never . . .!'

'I don't know, Gordon. First Mummy's brooch. Now my earrings. And Mrs Jinks *was* in the cupboard.'

Joe was half-crouching in the darkness, trying to hear the words through the thick wood. A floorboard creaked just behind him and he spun round as a hand reached out and touched his arm. For a horrible moment he had thought it was Granny, but in fact it was Mrs Jinks who had just come down the stairs. Joe opened his mouth to speak but she touched a finger to her lips and beckoned him back upstairs.

Mrs Jinks led him all the way to the top of the house. Only when she was back in her room with the door shut did she speak.

'Really, Joe!' she scolded him. 'I'm sure I've told you something about listening at doors.'

Joe sighed. 'I was only . . .'

'I know what you were doing. And it doesn't matter. Sit down.'

Joe sat down on the bed. Mrs Jinks sat beside him.

'Listen, my dear,' she began. 'I don't want to worry you but I think we ought to have a little talk—and I'm not sure if I'll have another opportunity.'

'You're not leaving, are you, Mrs Jinks?'

'No, no, no. Not unless I have to. But I wanted to have a word with you about your granny. Just in case . . .'

Mrs Jinks took a deep breath.

'Did I ever tell you about my time in the Amazon basin?' she asked at last. 'That time when I went to release my snake back into the wild?'

'Anna, an anaconda!' Joe exclaimed. Mrs Jinks had often spoken of her snake.

'That's right. Well, I wanted to release her as far away from civilization as I could. People are funny about

59

snakes and I couldn't bear to think of her ending up as a handbag or a pair of shoes or something. So I went to the town of Iquitos, which is on the Amazon river, and paid a fisherman to take me by canoe into the Amazon jungle.

'We sailed for three days, Anna, me and the fisherman. I can't begin to describe that jungle to you. I've never seen anything like it before—so green and so heavy and so silent. You could feel it pressing in on you on all sides. All that vegetation! Only a river as mighty as the Amazon could have managed to find a way through.

'On the third day we turned off into a tributary. By now the town was a long way behind us. There were no huts or anything and I was certain that Anna would be safe. So I took her out of her basket, gave her a kiss, and released her—'

'But what's this got to do with Granny?' Joe asked.

'You'll find out if you don't interrupt!' Mrs Jinks paused. 'Anna had gone,' she went on, 'and I was sitting there in the middle of a clearing feeling rather sorry for myself when suddenly . . .' She swallowed. 'Suddenly the biggest crocodile you've ever seen burst out of the undergrowth and lurched towards me. It must have been at least five metres long. Its scales weren't green (like they are in some of your old picture books) but an ugly grey. And it had the most terrible teeth. Razor sharp and quite revolting. Obviously it had never seen a dentist in its life and if it had it had probably eaten him.'

'How come it didn't eat you?' Joe asked.

'Oh, it tried to. But fortunately I was holding my umbrella and managed to force it into the creature's mouth, between its upper and its lower jaw. But that's not the point.'

Mrs Jinks drew Joe closer to her.

'I have never forgotten that crocodile's eyes, the way it looked at me. And not long ago I saw another pair of eyes just like them. Exactly the same. And I'm ashamed to say, Joe, that it was your granny's eyes at that tea party of hers. I saw them and quite frankly I would have preferred to have been sitting down with the crocodile.'

'So you believe me!' Joe whispered.

'I'm afraid I do.'

'But what can we do?'

'There's nothing I can do,' Mrs Jinks said, 'except to warn you to look after yourself. And remember this, Joe. In the end, the truth will always come out, no matter how long it takes.'

Joe pulled away. 'You're talking as if you're not going to stay!' he cried.

Mrs Jinks looked at him tiredly. 'I don't know,' she said. 'I really don't know. But I had to talk to you, Joe. Before it was too late . . .'

*   *   *

The next theft took place on the following Sunday. This time it was Mr Warden who was the victim. He had dozed off in his chair after lunch and when he woke up he knew at once that something was wrong. And it was. Someone had stolen two of his gold teeth.

'It'th a thcandal!' he cried out, whistling at the same time. There was a large gap at the front of his mouth. 'Thith ith a matter for the polithe!'

Granny, of course, was there. As Mr Warden raged and whistled, she shook her head as if she were utterly confused. 'Who would want to take two gold teeth?' she asked. 'Although now I think about it, Mrs Jinks was telling me how very much she admired them . . .'

After that, things happened very fast.

The police arrived in two police cars and an unmarked van. This, when it was opened, revealed two of the most ferocious dogs Joe had seen in his life. They were Alsatians, long-haired with thin, angular bodies and evil black eyes. Their tongues were drooling as they began to pad around the house, sniffing suspiciously.

'There's no meat out, is there?' the dog handler asked.

'Meat? No!' Mrs Warden replied.

'Good. It's just that Sherlock and Bones here haven't eaten for five days. It keeps them keen. But I can't let them get a smell of meat.'

63

'Please, officer,' Mrs Warden gestured. 'My husband is in here . . .'

The policemen followed her through into the living-room. Irma and Wolfgang went back to the west wing leaving Joe and Mrs Jinks in the hall. Mrs Jinks was looking rather pale.

'I think I'll go and sit outside,' she said. 'I need the fresh air.'

As she moved away, Joe heard a door softly close. Had someone been watching them? Granny? Suddenly worried, without knowing why, he opened the door and followed the passage on the other side all the way down to the kitchen.

There was someone there. Afraid of being seen, he peered round the corner just in time to see Granny climbing down from a cupboard with something in her hand. Now she was moving rapidly towards him and Joe ducked into the larder to hide. He heard a swish of material and caught a whiff of Decomposing Sheep as she passed but then she was gone. What was she doing? What had she taken?

Joe waited until he was sure she had

gone before he went back out into the hall but now there was no sign of her. In the living-room, he could hear his father talking to one of the policemen.

'Yeth, offither. They were thtolen when I wath athleep!'

He went back to the front door and looked out. Mrs Jinks was sitting on a bench at the side of the house and as he watched her, Joe heard a window open on the first floor. He wanted to call out to her but suddenly the two police dogs appeared, lumbering across the lawn, and he shrunk back.

But not before he had seen . . .

Something was drifting onto Mrs Jinks. At first Joe thought it was raining. But whatever it was was brown. And it was some sort of powder. Mrs Jinks hadn't noticed. She was sitting quietly, deep in thought. The powder sprinkled onto her shoulders, her lap, her hair.

And then the police dogs stopped, their bodies rigid. As Joe stared in horror, their eyes lit up and the hair on their backs began to bristle. The one called Sherlock began to growl. The other one—Bones—was panting; short, quick breaths that rasped in its throat.

Slowly, silently, the two of them closed in on Mrs Jinks.

'Hello, doggies . . .' Mrs Jinks had seen them. She stood up, noticing for the first time the brown powder that covered her arms and legs. She smelled it. And that must have been when she knew. The colour drained out of her face. Then she screamed, turned and ran.

'Sherlock! Bones!' The police dog handler had seen what was happening but too late. Like two bolts fired from a crossbow, the dogs took off after Mrs Jinks who had already sprinted across the lawn, through an ornamental pond, and who was now making for the bushes.

'Heel!' the police dog handler cried.

One of the police dogs bit Mrs Jinks's heel.

Mrs Jinks screamed again and disappeared into the bushes. With a terrible snarling and snapping the dogs fell on top of her.

Joe had watched all this in horror

and the rest was just a whirl. He vaguely remembered the policemen racing across the lawn when it was already far too late. He heard them all shouting as they blamed each other for what had happened. Someone must have called an ambulance, for a few minutes later one arrived, but then the stretcher bearers refused to get out until the dogs had been chained and muzzled. He saw Sherlock and Bones being led back to the police van, their heads hanging in disgrace, and saw, with a wave of despair, that they looked a lot fatter than they had been when they arrived.

Later on, he heard—and somehow he wasn't surprised—that the cameo brooch, the earrings and the two gold teeth had all been found in Mrs Jinks's room. They had, however, found nothing of Mrs Jinks apart from a few blood-stained scraps of clothing.

But for Joe, the very worst memory of the day, the one that would keep him awake all of that night and most of the next was of something he had seen in the middle of all the activity. As he stood in the hall he had heard something and had turned round just in time to see Granny coming down the stairs. At that moment, with just the two of them there, the mask was off again and the crocodile smile that Mrs Jinks had described was there for him to see.

But it wasn't the smile that frightened Joe. It was what Granny was holding in her hand, what she had taken from the kitchen a few minutes before.

It was a box of Bisto gravy powder.

Without saying a word, Granny hurried past him and went into the kitchen to put it back.

GRANNY MOVES IN

Nobody felt the death of Mrs Jinks more keenly than Joe. It was as if he had lost his only friend—which, in a way, he had. And not only was she dead but she had been branded a thief and that hurt him all the more. 'The truth will always come out.' That was what she had said to him. But how could he go to his parents or the police and tell them that it was Granny who had taken the jewellery and the gold teeth and that it was she who had killed Mrs Jinks by pouring gravy powder over her when the police dogs were near because . . . because . . . What reason could there possibly be? They would think he was mad.

Every day when he got home from school, Joe found himself on his own. He took to walking down to the bottom of the garden where Mr Lampy would be waiting for him and the two of them would sit together next to a burning brazier with the family of moles watching them through the window of the shed.

'I'm going to run away,' he would say. 'I'll go to China and work in a paddy-field.'

'I don't know, Master Warden,' Mr Lampy would reply. 'China's a long way away. And who's this Paddy you're talking about?'

Meanwhile, Mr and Mrs Warden had problems of their own. The summer holiday was about to start and that meant the departure of Wolfgang and Irma. Every year the cook and her husband went home to Hungary although, as they only owned a caravan just outside Budapest, Mr Warden would have much preferred it if the home had come to them. What it meant was that for three weeks there would be no cook and no butler. Worse still, Mrs Warden had been unable to find a new nanny to look after Joe even though she'd advertised. The fact that the last nanny had just been eaten by two dogs probably didn't help.

'We've got to find someone to look

after Jordan,' Mrs Warden said the night after Wolfgang and Irma had gone.

'What? What did you say?' Mr Warden was lying in bed, smoking a cigar and reading *The Economist.*

Mrs Warden pivoted round upside down. She had recently begun a course in escapology and as well as being hand-cuffed, strait-jacketed and sellotaped, she was also tied by one foot to the chandelier. 'I said we've got to find someone to look after Jordan.'

'Oh yes. But who?'

'I was thinking about Mr Lampy.'

'Mr Lampy? He's just the gardener. And he's over eighty. Completely senile . . .'

Mrs Warden tugged with her teeth at one of the ropes that bound her. It wouldn't give. 'We could ask Mabel Butterworth. She's an angel.'

'You're absolutely right,' Mr Warden said. 'She died two years ago.'

'Did she?' Mrs Warden blinked. 'No wonder she hasn't been returning my calls.' She considered for a moment. 'How about Barbara Finegold? She always says how much she likes kids.'

'But she means goats,' Mr Warden said. 'She's always had a fondness for goats. She keeps two of the brutes as pets.'

'Well, there must be someone.'

'How about you?' Mr Warden suggested. 'After all, you are the boy's mother.'

'I hadn't thought of that,' Mrs Warden muttered. 'I suppose it is an idea . . . I mean, I could look after him for a few days.'

Mrs Warden twisted round again, trying to release a hand from the strait-jacket without dislocating her shoulder. Nothing happened. 'This isn't working,' she sighed. 'I'm sorry, Gordon, but I'm afraid you're going to have to untie me. Gordon? Gordon . . . ?'

But Mr Warden had fallen sound asleep.

The next day did not begin well. Mrs Warden had a headache (from sleeping upside down) and had no wish to be left alone with Joe. Mr Warden had left early for the office even though—as

Mrs Warden realized an hour after he was gone—it was Saturday. Joe was waiting for her in the kitchen, studying a map of China.

'Good morning, Jordan,' she said.

Joe looked up. He had been thinking about life in Chwannping.

'Now,' Mrs Warden went on. 'I'm just going to make you some breakfast. Then I'm afraid I have a hair appointment and then my bridge lesson with Dr Vitebski. This week we're learning about suspension bridges. So will you be all right on your own until lunch?'

Joe nodded.

'Good.' Mrs Warden was in a hurry. She threw a spoonful of coffee granules into her mouth and sipped some boiling water from the kettle. 'I'd love to have lunch with you,' she went on, 'but I'm meeting Jane for elevenses and as she's always late it's bound to be twelveses. The poor dear is all at sixes and sevens! Maybe I'll buy her some After Eights.'

Joe had lost count trying to work this out but his mother went on anyway.

'I'm going shopping this afternoon,' she said. 'I thought I'd go to the spring sales. The sofa in the living-room needs some new springs. Then tea at the Ritz and I should be home in time for supper.'

'Do you want me to make the supper?' Joe asked.

'I don't think so, darling!' Mrs Warden giggled. 'Leave that to me!'

But in fact she was so exhausted after her day's shopping that she quite forgot to cook. That evening, Mr Warden and Joe sat at the table staring gloomily at three tins of pink salmon. Mrs Warden was even gloomier. She couldn't find the tin opener.

'This house is going to the dogs!' Mr Warden muttered. 'And I'm going to a hotel!'

Mrs Warden burst into tears. 'It's not my fault,' she wept. 'I've been so busy! How can I be expected to do everything?'

'Well, is there *no* food in the house?' Mr Warden asked.

'There was a chicken and some peas.'

'You could at least have cooked the peas,' Mr Warden growled.

'I tried to. But the chicken ate them. And then I tried to cook the chicken but it ran away.'

The days without Wolfgang and Irma crawled slowly by. Mrs Warden filled the house with ready meals. Mr Warden spent longer and longer at the office. And Joe began to teach himself Chinese. But quite rapidly things began to fall apart.

On Tuesday night the dishwasher broke down, much to the horror of Mrs Warden, who hadn't washed a dish herself since 1963 (and then she had only rinsed it). The next day she went out and bought a hundred paper plates which were fine with the main courses and puddings but caused problems with the soup. On Wednesday, Mr Warden attempted to dry his shoes by placing them in the microwave. His feet were actually glowing as he took the tube to work and he caused a bomb scare at Charing Cross. On Thursday, the toaster exploded when Mr Warden tried to light it with a match. On Friday it was the Hoover. Mrs Warden only just escaped a terrible injury when she tried to use it to blow-dry her hair.

You may think it pathetic that Mr and Mrs Warden were so incapable of looking after themselves but you'd be surprised how true this is of the very rich. They've been looked after by servants for so long that they don't know how to do anything for themselves. Ask the Queen what a Brillo pad is and she'd probably tell you it was a lovely place to live.

Anyway, as the week progressed, the house became dustier and dirtier and more broken down. Joe for the most part avoided his parents and spent most of his time with Mr Lampy.

Chinese had proved impossible to learn so he was thinking now about volunteering for the American shuttle to Mars.

And then, on Saturday, Granny came to lunch.

'You know, Maud, darling,' she said, munching on a mouthful of Marks and Spencer's Instant Saturday Lunch, 'you and Gordon look terribly tired.'

'I am tired!' Mr Warden muttered.

'Don't you usually go to the south of France at this time of the year?'

'We can't, Mumsy,' Mrs Warden sighed.

'Why ever not?' Granny had hardly glanced at Joe, sitting opposite her at the table, but he was suddenly suspicious. Granny knew perfectly well that his parents had a flat in Cannes. She also knew that the flat only had one bedroom.

'What about Jordan?' Mrs Warden said.

'I'm sure he'd love to go with you.'

'There's no room,' Mr Warden muttered.

'Well . . .' There was a pause. 'I could look after him while you were away.'

Joe's mouth went dry. One after another the hairs on the back of his neck stood up. Alone with Granny? He'd prefer to be alone with a sabre-toothed tiger.

'I could move in, if you wanted me to,' she went on. Her whole face had gone rubbery and there was a sweetness in her voice. But Joe could see her eyes. They were still sly. 'Joe would love it. Wouldn't you, dear?'

'Aaagh!' Joe yelled. For even as Granny had spoken the words, he had felt a terrible explosion of pain. Under the table, a leather-capped shoe had just come into hard contact with his knee.

'I'm sorry, dear?' Granny gazed at him enquiringly.

'You can't!' Joe gasped.

'What?' Mr Warden was furious. 'Your granny offers to look after you and that's all you can say?'

'I mean . . . I mean, it isn't fair on Granny.' Joe was blushing now. Could he tell the truth? That was what Mrs Jinks had advised but looking at his parents now he knew it was impossible. He forced himself to think. 'I'd love to be with Granny,' he went on. 'But wouldn't it be too much work for her? It might make her ill.'

'Oh, silly me!' Granny trilled. 'I've dropped my fork!' She disappeared under the table.

'Wait a minute . . .' Joe began.

'What is the matter with you,

Jordan?' his mother asked.

A second later, Joe jerked upright in his seat as three metal prongs buried themselves in his thigh. He had been holding a glass of water but now he cried out, his hand jerked and the water sprayed over his father, putting out his cigar.

'Have you gone mad?' Mr Warden demanded.

'No, father, I . . .' Joe put down the glass and reached under the table. There were three holes in his trousers—not to mention in his leg.

'I'll look after him.' Granny was already back in her seat. For someone so old, she had moved incredibly fast. 'It would only be for a few weeks. I'm sure we'd have a lot of fun . . .'

Joe stared at her. Granny leaned forward and picked up the bread knife: thirteen inches of serrated steel. She looked at him and smiled. Joe shrank back into his chair. When he spoke, his voice was thin and high-pitched. 'What about Mr Lampy?' he quavered.

'What about him?' his mother said.

'He's a lot younger than Granny.

Couldn't he look after me? That way, you and father could have your holiday, Granny wouldn't have to bother about me and everyone would be happy.'

Across the table, Granny was gripping the bread knife so tightly that her fingers had gone white and the veins were wriggling under her skin like worms. Joe held his breath, his eyes fixed on the knife.

'I did suggest Mr Lampy,' Mrs Warden said.

'Maybe it's not such a bad idea,' Mr Warden muttered.

'I think it's a very good idea . . .'

Granny put down the knife. Her lips had gone all wobbly and there were tears brimming in her eyes like rainwater in the folds of a tent. 'Well, if you don't want me,' she burbled. 'If you don't like me . . .'

'Of course he likes you, Mummy,' Mrs Warden said. 'Jordan was just worried about you, that's all.'

'I certainly was,' Joe agreed.

'Well, all right.' Granny forced herself to cheer up. 'You two get your tickets then and have a lovely time.'

But then her eyes narrowed and the next words were aimed directly at Joe. 'And if anything terrible happens to Mr Lampy, if he's unlucky enough to have a dreadful accident in the next few days, just you let me know.'

*   *   *

'Now don't you worry about me, Master Warden,' Mr Lampy said.

It was the morning before Mr and Mrs Warden were about to leave. Mr Lampy had just come out of the shed carrying a canister of petrol. He had been cutting back the shrubbery at the bottom of the garden and was about to light a bonfire.

'You and me . . . we're going to get along all right.'

'That's not what I'm worried about,' Joe replied. 'It's Granny . . .'

'You and your granny!' Mr Lampy set the canister down and rubbed the small of his back. 'Ooh!' he exclaimed. 'I been to see the doctor today and he goes on about someone called Arthur Itis. Arthur Itis? I never heard of him.'

'Please, Mr Lampy . . .'

Mr Lampy smiled. He was a very old man and when he smiled his face folded into a hundred creases. He had spent his whole life out of doors. In ten years in the Navy he had never once gone below deck—all the more remarkable when you consider that he served on a submarine. 'I haven't seen your granny and I don't intend to see her,' he went on. He leaned down and picked up the petrol canister. 'I reckon she'll be leaving the two of us alone.'

Joe watched as Mr Lampy walked away. He wasn't convinced but there seemed to be no point in arguing any more. The last thing he saw of Mr Lampy was the old gardener leaning over a great pile of wood-cuttings and leaves, sprinkling it with petrol from the canister. He didn't see Mr Lampy light the match.

The explosion could be heard thirty miles away and at first the police thought it was a terrorist attack. Like Mrs Jinks before him, nothing was found of Mr Lampy—which was hardly surprising. He had blown a crater five metres deep in the earth. Four trees, the rockery, the garden shed and the moles went with him, blown into so many pieces that it was quite impossible to say what belonged to what. One question puzzled everyone. How had Mr Lampy managed to sprinkle nitro-glycerine on his bonfire? And how had it got into what should have been a canister of petrol?

The investigation led nowhere. One witness did come forward claiming that he had seen a figure climbing over the fence into the garden of Thattlebee Hall. But as the witness had been on his way back from the pub and as he insisted that the figure he had seen had been a woman, and one who was over ninety years old, his evidence was discounted.

A few days later, Mr and Mrs Warden left for their flat in the south of France.

The same day, Granny moved in.

GATHERING OF THE GRANNIES

Breakfast was cream cheese.

Lunch was cream cheese.

Tea was more cream cheese.

After just one day, Joe was the colour of cream cheese. The house had never felt so big and he had never felt so small. His parents were away in another country. Mrs Jinks and Mr Lampy were dead. There was just Joe and Granny and he knew with a horrible sick feeling in the pit of his stomach that he was completely in her power.

Of course, Granny was enjoying every minute of it, moving round the house, warbling to herself like a sick canary as she glued shut the windows and turned up the heating. By lunch-time Joe was sweating.

'You look ill, dear,' Granny trilled.

'I'm hot.'

'It must be the flu. You'd better have two spoonfuls of cod-liver oil. Better still, I'll go to the fishmongers and buy you a whole cod's liver.'

That afternoon, Mr and Mrs Warden telephoned from the south of France. Although Joe was in the room, they didn't ask to speak to him. Instead, Mrs Warden gabbled down the phone to Granny at twice her usual speed. She always did this to save money on long-distance calls.

'Are you sure everything's all right, Mumsy?' she asked.

'Don't you worry, dear. Jasper and I are having a wonderful time. He's no trouble at all!'

'There is one thing, Mummy. Could you put an advert in *The Lady* for a new nanny? We'll have to have one when we get back.'

'Oh, Jack won't be needing a new nanny . . .' Joe heard the words. They sent a shiver down his spine.

'Mummy . . . ?'

Granny was holding the telephone in a claw-like hand. She smiled into it. 'Lovely talking to you, dear. Must go!' The smile evaporated. Granny hung up.

Granny made a number of telephone calls after that but Joe was pretty certain that none of them were to *The Lady*. She was careful to close the door before she began but Joe did manage to hear her checking train times with British Rail and so assumed that she— and presumably he with her—was about to go away.

This was confirmed at the end of the day. Joe had eaten his supper on his own and was settling down to watch television when the door opened and Granny came in.

'Bedtime, Jane, dear!'

'I'm Joe! And it's only eight o'clock. I never go to bed before nine.'

'Don't argue with Granny. Granny knows best!'

'But I'm watching *The Bill*!'

'So am I, dear.' Granny flicked the television off. 'The electricity bill—and that should save a bit! Now up to bed!'

But the torment didn't even stop there. Although it was a warm night, Granny had insisted on his wearing a vest as well as his pyjamas, a dressing-gown as well as a vest and two extra blankets on top of everything else.

'We don't want your flu to get any worse, do we, dear,' she said when she came into his room.

'I can't sleep like this,' Joe said. 'I feel like a sausage roll!'

'You can't have a sausage roll now, dear,' Granny replied. 'But maybe I'll get you one tomorrow.' And with a soft giggle, she switched off the light and went out.

Joe lay in bed for a long time. He was too hot to sleep and also too angry. As he lay in the half-darkness, he began to think about how unfair life was. He was twelve (almost thirteen) years old. He could read, write, add up, speak French, swim, juggle and name over a thousand characters in science fiction books and films. But did he have any life of his own? No! His every movement was controlled and organized by adults with less imagination than him. His parents, the teachers at his posh prep school—they were all the same, passing him around as if he were no more than a tin of sweets. Of course, it wouldn't be so bad if the grown-ups had more sense. But nobody had to be qualified to be a parent. And his parents were not only unqualified, they had quite happily handed him to a woman who hated him and who in the last few weeks had just killed his two best friends. But who would believe him? Nobody!

If he hadn't been so hot and angry, maybe he would have slept. But he was still awake at nine o'clock when the doorbell rang. He was awake at ten past nine when it rang again. And he had given up any idea of sleeping by half past when it rang for a third time.

As the evening dragged on, Joe began to hear strange sounds coming from downstairs. The hiss of a can being opened and a peal of high-pitched laughter. A clink of glasses and the slam of a cupboard door. More laughter. There seemed to be four or five women downstairs. The muffled sound of arguing and then another cackle of laughter drifted up to his room. In the end he couldn't bear it any longer. He got up and went downstairs.

The hall was dark but the door to the living-room was half open which was how the sounds had escaped. Thankful for his bare feet and the thick carpets, Joe tiptoed forward and peeped in. An extraordinary sight met his eyes.

There were five grannies in the room, playing poker. They had assembled a green baize card table and had two decks of cards scattered over the surface, on the floor and—in at least two instances—up their sleeves. The room was thick with smoke. Two of the grannies were smoking cigarettes while a third had helped herself to one of Mr Warden's cigars. They had opened half a dozen cans of beer and a bottle of whisky. There were glasses everywhere. Granny had also provided food. There was a bowl of popcorn, some bright pink hot dogs with fried onions and American mustard, a plate of pickled cucumbers, two boxes of Fortnum and Mason chocolates, some salt beef sandwiches and several packets of chewing gum. Joe wasn't at all surprised that there wasn't an ounce of cream cheese in sight.

But what made the spectacle so bizarre as well as so revolting was the old ladies themselves. Their combined ages must have added up to well over four hundred. Joe had once seen a few minutes of a video called *Revenge of the Killer Zombies.* It had given him nightmares for a week. Well, this was far, far worse.

Granny One was a small, shrivelled woman, no more than four feet high. Her head barely came over the edge of the table and she was blinking at the cards in her hand with small, pink eyes. She seemed to be finding it difficult to balance on her chair—perhaps because of the enormous amount of jewellery she was wearing and the bulging handbag she was clutching to her chest. This granny's hands were everywhere at once: holding her cards (and trying to stop her neighbour seeing them), guarding her bag, tilting her whisky glass towards her lips and poking her nose and ears. Look quickly, and you might think she had four arms. Her name was Granny Anne.

Granny Two was wearing what looked like a pair of curtains—but they were curtains you would draw at your peril. For this granny was immensely fat. She was so fat that she seemed to have partially melted into her chair. She was obviously a careful poker player as she was keeping her cards close to her chin—or rather, chins, for she had three of them. The third of these was crowned with a wispy beard. Granny Two was sucking a hot dog. She couldn't eat it as, for extra comfort, she had removed her false teeth and placed them in front of her on the table. Her name was Granny Smith.

The first things Joe noticed about Granny Three were her quite horrible eyes. She was wearing a heavy pair of spectacles which, over the years, had stretched her ears and sunk into her nose. In fact her entire face was lop-sided and she hadn't helped it by putting on too much lipstick—at the same time missing her lips. Her eyeballs, magnified by what looked like inch-thick glass, were a milky shade of white with one a little higher than the other. Granny Three was smoking, eating, drinking and talking all at the same time. And all the time she was watching. Her eyes, darting about in her drooping sockets, missed nothing. She answered to the name of Granny Adams.

Granny Four, shovelling enormous handfuls of popcorn into her mouth, was a vulture. She had the same long neck, bald head and cruel eyes. And she was wearing a flowing green cloak mounted with feathers which added to the illusion. This was the granny who was smoking the cigar. She was using it to point with and as Joe watched, the glowing tip caught Granny Smith on the chin. Granny Smith cried out and fell backwards, two aces tumbling out of her jacket. Granny Adams threw a glass of beer at her and screamed with laughter while Granny Anne pounded the table and chewed gum. This last granny was called Granny Lee.

Dominating the table was Granny herself, looking almost royal in a billowing dress with flouncy neck and sleeves. She was sitting with her arms and legs apart and a scowl on her face. Suddenly she threw her cards down.

'A full house. Kings high. Beat that!' She announced.

'I've got a pair of twos,' Granny Anne exclaimed in a quavering voice.

Granny Smith grabbed them and tore them up. 'You lose, Anne. Two twos aren't worth anything.'

'Well, I've got another two in my bra,' Anne exclaimed.

'Cheat! Cheat! Cheat!' Granny Adams screeched with laughter. 'I haven't got anything,' she added and threw her cards in a shower over her head.

'Well, I've got a royal flush,' the vulture granny snapped. 'Ace, king, queen, knave, ten.' She spread the cards on the table.

'How did you do that?' Granny scrabbled at the cards, examining them as if they were forgeries. Her face had gone dark red. 'You've been cheating as well, haven't you, Lee?'

'Of course I've been cheating,' Granny Lee replied. 'We've all been cheating. But I've just been cheating better than you.'

'Well, how much do I owe you?' Granny was sulking now, her lip jutting out and her shoulders slumped.

'Let me see . . .' Granny Lee scribbled a few figures on a sheet of paper. 'That's two shillings and fourpence.'

'How much is that in new money?' Granny Anne asked nervously.

'We don't have nasty new money here, Anne,' Granny replied. She brought her elbow up sharply, catching the little granny in the eye. 'Two shillings and fourpence is just what it says it is.'

'Oh! Lovely old money!' Granny Smith sighed, her three chins rising and falling in perfect unison. 'It used to be worth something once, money did. I could buy dinner for three people with two shillings and fourpence.'

'Yes,' Granny Lee snapped. 'But the trouble was, you'd eat it all yourself!' And her whole body shook as she laughed uncontrollably.

Meanwhile Granny had gathered in

the torn and crumpled cards and was once again shuffling the pack.

'So tell me, Ivy,' Granny Anne asked. 'What's the news about that grandson of yours?'

At the door, Joe froze.

'Yes!' Granny Adams rubbed her hands together. Her eyes rolled like two worms in walnut shells. 'How are his enzymes?'

'Enzymes! Enzymes!' Granny Lee and Granny Anne chorused.

Granny held up a hand. 'You'll find out soon enough,' she rasped. 'I'm taking him with me tomorrow.'

'What?' The other grannies stared in amazement and delight.

'Can you?' Granny Smith asked. 'What about his parents?'

'They're not here,' Granny replied. 'Anyway, they don't care a jot about him. They won't even notice.'

'Do you mean . . .' Granny Lee twisted her neck until the bones clicked. 'You've got him all to yourself?'

Granny nodded. 'Yes. I've had quite a bit of fun at his expense, I can tell you.' She licked her lips and began to deal. 'But maybe I'm getting old. I feel I haven't quite made him miserable enough!'

Joe felt the hairs on the back of his neck prickle. If only he could have tape-recorded this conversation—his parents would have had to believe him. He'd guessed that Granny hated him. Now he had the proof of it. But all that talk of enzymes worried him. What were they planning? Where was he going to be taken?

'How I hate children!' the vulture granny moaned.

'Me too!'

'I can't stand them.'

'I detest them!'

All the grannies were nodding so vigorously that Joe wouldn't have been surprised if their heads had come loose from their necks and rolled across the surface of the card table.

'You know what I hate about them?' Granny Smith said. 'I hate their perfect skin. It's all pink and shiny and smooth. I hate their hair, so thick and wavy. But most of all I hate their teeth.' She gazed at her own on the table in front of her. 'Do you know where children keep their teeth? In their mouths! It isn't fair.'

'I hate children because they're so healthy,' Granny Anne went on. 'They're always shouting and playing and having fun and running about. I haven't run anywhere since 1958 and that was only for a bus.'

'I hate them because of everything they've got,' Granny Adams muttered. 'We never had computers and pop music and T-shirts and mountain bikes. But they have. I fought in two world wars but nobody ever gave me a skateboard. Oh no!'

'Children smell,' Granny Lee announced. 'They're too small and they make too much noise. Why can't they be more like us?'

'Yes. With arthritis!'

'And swollen knees.'

'Hard of hearing!'

'What?'

'And wrinkly.'

'Horrid! Horrid! Horrid! Horrid! Horrid!' All five grannies were chorusing together now and pounding their fists on the table at the same time. Joe couldn't believe what he was seeing. It seemed that the five old ladies had gone quite mad.

At last Granny stopped them.

'But we can at least get our revenge,' she said. 'There are so many ways to upset a grandchild.'

'Oh, yes!' Granny Adams giggled. Her glasses jumped up and down on her nose. 'When I see my grandchildren, I always poke them a lot. I do find that children hate being poked.'

'I don't just poke them,' the little granny said. 'I pat them on their heads and fiddle with their clothes. It does annoy them so, although of course they're not allowed to complain.'

'And don't forget the kiss!' Granny Smith said. 'The wet kiss on the cheek makes them squirm like frogs in a pond!'

'What about presents?' Granny asked. 'Presents are a marvellous way of spoiling any child's day.'

'Oh, yes! A boring book token!'

'Talcum powder!'

'Something you know they've already got!'

'What I do,' Granny said, 'is buy them something that's too young for them. Something that will make them feel babyish.

They feel so ashamed. It's hilarious.'

(At the door, Joe remembered the toy robot and found that his face was burning once again. But this time it wasn't with embarrassment. It was anger.)

'I have a much better idea,' Granny Lee said. 'I buy my grandchildren hideously unsuitable clothes. I've managed to find some of the most ghastly pullovers in the world.'

'I knit them myself,' Granny Anne muttered.

'The children *have* to wear them,' Granny Lee went on. 'And you should see them! I always take them out to tea and watch their faces as they walk out in their horrible, huge, brightly-coloured jumpers . . .'

'I've got a much better idea,' Granny Adams interjected. 'My grandchildren are a little overweight. So guess what I buy them—chocolates! I get them a whole box and of course they eat them and that just makes them fatter and spottier and when they go back to school they're terribly teased and all thanks to me. You should try the chocolate wheeze! The little brats can never resist a chocolate.'

'It seems to me that you should combine the two ideas,' Granny said. 'Give them the chocolates. And give them a jersey that's a little too small. Then, when their tummies are bulging it will really show.'

The other four grannies thought about this and then all shrieked with laughter. More glasses of whisky were poured. More beer cans were cracked open. The fat granny was laughing so much that her whole body was convulsing and her face had gone bright red.

Joe couldn't bear any more. He took three steps away from the door, shrinking into the shadows of the hall. But even as he went he heard his name once again being bounced around the card table.

'So you're going to take the boy?'

'Oh, yes. He's coming. I've had my eye on him for a long time.'

'Which eye, dear? The real one or the glass one?'

'Have you spoken to . . . Elsie Bucket?' This was Granny Lee's voice. She had spoken the name with awe.

'Oh, yes. I spoke to Elsie. She's delighted.'

'Delighted!'

'Excited!'

'Enzymes!'

'Hee hee hee . . .'

The five of them were like witches. Add a cauldron and a few frogs and there would have been no difference. Joe turned and tiptoed back the way he had come. The voices followed him as he made his way back to bed.

THE GOLDEN GRANNY AWARDS

'Pack your bags, Judas. We're going on holiday.'

It was breakfast the following day and Joe had just come downstairs to find Granny tucking into a plate of eggs, bacon, sausage, tomatoes, fried bread and black pudding. She had prepared a half grapefruit topped with a small amount of cream cheese for him.

'Where are we going?' Joe asked. He knew she was always getting his name wrong on purpose and decided not to correct her.

'To Bideford in Devonshire. It's a delightful town. I spent many happy years there in the war.'

'The Crimean War, Granny?'

'There's no need to be rude, dear.' Granny lashed out with a curiously powerful fist. If Joe hadn't ducked at the last moment she would have broken his chin. Even so he felt the air as it punched past him. 'It was the

Second World War. Ah, what happy days those were. Rationing and bombs and dried eggs for breakfast. Your grandfather got blown to smithereens in the Second World War. Such happy days!'

'I don't want to go to Bideford,' Joe said, sitting on the edge of his chair in case he had to duck a second blow.

'I'm sure you don't, dear,' Granny simpered. 'But you're twelve and I'm ninety-four. So you don't really have any choice.'

'I could ring Mum and Dad . . .'

'And drag them all the way back from France? I don't think they'd be very pleased. Anyway, I've already told them I'm taking you.' She smiled unpleasantly.

'Why are you doing this, Granny?' Joe demanded. 'What do you want?'

Granny paused with her fork inches from her mouth. Egg white dangled greasily in front of her lips. Suddenly she was innocent again. 'I want to look after you,' she said. 'Just like any granny would.'

* * *

The taxi dropped them at Paddington
Station and the driver scowled as
Granny counted out the fare in one,
two and five-penny pieces. It took her
ten minutes to pay by which time the
driver was covered in coins.

'Seven pounds twenty pence?' she
demanded. 'There you are! That's
seven pounds twenty-one. Keep the
change!'

Joe grabbed the suitcases and
Granny grabbed Joe and together they
made their way through the station
concourse. As they walked, Joe saw
something rather strange. A woman
had got out of the taxi just behind
them—he had noticed her out of the
corner of his eye because he had
thought he recognized her—and now
she seemed to be following them.
Nervously, he glanced over his
shoulder. She was still there, her face
almost completely hidden by a scarf
over her mouth and a pair of dark
glasses over her eyes. A lock of blonde

hair poked out from under a voluminous hat and she walked with a pronounced limp. Where had Joe seen her before?

But maybe he was imagining the whole thing. For when he looked around again a few moments later, the mysterious woman had gone.

Granny checked her ticket and pointed at a train. There was a guard standing beside it, leaning against it with one hand splayed out on the metal surface and the other hand in his pocket. The guard hadn't shaved that morning. There was a cigarette behind his ear.

'Excuse me . . .' Granny said.

The guard looked at her with a syrupy smile and almost at once Joe recognized the sort of man he was. He was just like his Uncle David, the sort of man who believes that all old people are like children, that they don't understand anything except simple words spoken loudly. Joe had always hated that sort of behaviour but now his interest was aroused. How would Granny react?

'Yes, my love. How *are* you today?' The guard shouted out the words. He was leaning over Granny, nodding his head at her.

Granny's lips tightened. 'Is this the train for Bideford?' she snapped.

'No, dear!' The guard was still shouting and he shook his head vigorously for good measure. 'There's no *station* at Bideford, darling. There hasn't been for twenty years! You have to go to *Barnstaple* and get a bus!'

'Is this the train for Barnstaple?' Granny demanded.

'Yes!' Now he nodded like a thirsty duck. He was showing all his teeth (and several fillings) in a wide smile. 'Can you get on all right, dear? Got a *ticket*, have you?'

'Of course I've got a ticket!'

'Good! Good! Now you change at *Exeter*, all right. Do you think you can remember that?'

'Yes.'

'That your grandson, is he? *He'll* look after you! Don't you worry, love. You'll be all right.'

The guard hadn't noticed but

Granny's cheeks had gone a dark red and her lips were so tight they could have been sewn together. She didn't say anything more but got on the train with Joe and found her seat. Then she looked at her watch.

'We've got ten minutes,' she muttered, as much to herself as him. 'You wait here. I'll be right back . . .'

As soon as Granny had gone, Joe slipped out of his seat and went over to the open door. He was curious. What was she going to do? He saw her scuttling across the concourse to the newsagent and a minute later she came out clutching something in her hand. Now she was hovering, waiting for something. Joe followed her eyes and saw the guard, still leaning against the train with his palm flat on the surface. Suddenly making up her mind, Granny moved towards him. She was going to do something, Joe was sure of it. But then a crowd of tourists appeared and for a minute, Joe's vision was blocked.

When he looked again, Granny was past the guard and walking back towards the train. The guard had been distracted by something but now he took his cigarette out, lit it and once again leaned against the train. Joe hurried back to his seat. He was sitting back with his eyes half-closed when Granny joined him.

Three minutes later, the train left.

Granny had brought a magazine with her but she didn't read it. She was smiling to herself with that odd, dangerous light in her eyes.

Joe glanced at her handbag, which lay half-open on the seat beside her. There was a torn carton inside. What was it she had bought in the newsagent? Joe read one single word and shuddered.

SUPERGLUE.

They were delayed for one hour at Reading while they prised the guard off the train. He had run the whole way from Paddington, one hand glued to the side of the carriage. He was taken to hospital by ambulance to be treated for exhaustion, multiple blisters and shock. Granny watched through the window as the ambulance left.

'I hate being patronized,' she said.

'Yes, Granny.'

For the rest of the journey, Joe kept his mouth firmly shut.

*   *   *

Bideford was pretty enough, stretched out along a harbour with a few fishing boats moored on the other side of the parking meters. The taxi had brought Joe and Granny all the way from Barnstaple and as it cruised along the High Street he noticed two things. The first was that every single shop in the town sold Devonshire clotted cream. And the second was that there seemed to be an unusually large number of elderly ladies in the street—all of them with knitted hats and shopping trolleys.

'No wonder it's called Bideford,' Joe thought to himself. 'The place is full of old biddies.'

The taxi turned right and followed a narrow, twisting road up a steep hill. At the top it stopped and Joe saw the hotel where they were staying.

It was a tall, double-fronted house, four floors high but with extra rooms built into the roof. The house was old but the owners had tried to modernize it with a revolving door (which looked ridiculous) and a white marble forecourt. The hotel advertised forty-five rooms 'all with hot and cold running water' except that someone had crossed out the 'and' and replaced it with 'or'. Apparently they had plumbing problems. It was called The Stilton International.

Granny paid the driver and she and Joe went in. The reception area was surprisingly large—the whole hotel seemed bigger inside than out.

While Granny checked in for both of them, Joe wandered between the artificial leather sofas and the wilting pot plants—the hotel was as hot as Granny's flat—and went over to a large sign on the opposite wall. It was made up of plastic letters, although some of the alphabet was evidently missing, and it read:

THE STILTON INTERNATIONAL

welcoMes grannies
TonigHt at 10.00pm in the
Elsie Bucket Conference Room
THe GOLDeN GRANNY AWARDS

'The Golden Granny Awards . . .' Joe muttered the words to himself and, looking around him, he suddenly realized—with a lurch in his stomach—that the hotel was occupied entirely by grannies. There were half a dozen of them sitting in the reception area reading magazines or nodding off to sleep. The lift arrived and three more grannies got out, whispering among themselves. Two grannies met on the forecourt and Joe heard them greet each other.

'Gladys!'

'Evelyn! I haven't seen you since . . . 1942!'

'Fifty-two years ago, Gladys! You haven't changed . . .'

'Haven't I, Evelyn, dear?'

'No! You're still wearing the same

dress.'

A coach had drawn up and another fifteen grannies got out and formed a queue at the reception, chatting excitedly among themselves. They were all carrying shopping trolleys and old, heavy suitcases. But now Joe noticed something else. It was very strange, but they had brought what looked like scientific equipment along with them too. One granny had a large test tube. Another had a Bunsen burner. A third granny had a series of twisting glass pipes while the granny behind her had some sort of electrical apparatus complete with copper wires, magnetic switches and complicated micro-circuitry. The last granny in the line was completely bowed down by something that could have come straight out of one of his science fiction books: it was like a glass and steel tuba with a whole series of levers and buttons and flashing lights. One of the other grannies was admiring it.

'You got an electro-static de-energizer!' she exclaimed. 'How lovely! Where did you find it?'

'My grandson's a nuclear physicist,' the other granny explained. 'He made it for me.'

'Did you tell him what it was for?'

'No. And fortunately he didn't ask.'

Not one single granny had looked at Joe. He was aware that he was the only person in the building under seventy (even the receptionist was white-haired). Normally he would have expected the grannies to tussle his hair or tug at his clothes. But it was as if they were actually avoiding him. He felt their eyes settle momentarily on him but then dart away. Nobody spoke to him. They seemed almost afraid of him.

Something poked Joe in the ribs and he spun round to find Granny dangling a key in front of him. 'Here you are, Jasper,' she said. 'You've got room 45. Go and unpack and I'll see you at dinner. And you be a good boy, now!'

Joe took the key and as his hand came into contact with the cold metal a shiver ran down his whole body. Granny's eyes had locked into his and for a moment he could see the hunger in them. He felt her eyes sucking him dry and at the same time the words 'electro-static de-energizer' echoed in his mind. What did it do? What was it for?

And why was he so sure that it had something to do with him?

*   *   *

Room 45 was at the *very* top of the hotel, built into the roof with slanting walls and a small, low window. Joe quickly unpacked then set out to explore the Stilton International. He had never been anywhere quite like it in his life.

In the basement there was a swimming-pool, but the water was so hot that the entire room was filled with steam and he could hardly see anything. But there were grannies there. He couldn't see them but he could hear them, cackling eerily in the steam and pattering across the tiled surface like ghosts.

Near the swimming-pool there was a beauty parlour and Joe stared through the open door as one of the grannies lay back in what looked like a dentist's chair. The beauty specialist was a small, foreign-looking man with a wig and a moustache that didn't quite match. The granny he was working on already had two cucumber slices on her eyes, two straws up her nose and a thick white cream on her lips.

'Oh yes, Mrs Grimstone,' he was saying. 'To bring out the beauty of the skin, to give it back its youth, it requires the natural products only.' He produced a bucket and scooped out a handful of something brown and steaming. 'That is why I use only the finest quality buffalo dung. Rich in minerals and vitamins. High in protein. It will draw out the natural colour.'

Joe moved away as the beauty specialist slapped the first handful of the stuff on Mrs Grimstone's cheek.

There was a fashion shop on the ground floor where Joe watched grannies trying on all sorts of brilliantly coloured clothes. One granny was standing in front of a mirror having squeezed herself—with great difficulty

—into an impossibly tight leopard-skin leotard with a black top and brilliant red head-band which now matched her brilliant red face.

'Gorgeous, Mrs Hodgson,' the shop assistant was crooning. 'Quite gorgeous! You don't look a day over eighty-five!'

Next to the fashion shop was a health food shop. The window was filled with pills and bottles, strange roots and powders . . . all of which were designed to make whoever swallowed them feel young again.

'I particularly recommend raw garlic and seaweed cocktail,' the owner was saying. 'Just two mouthfuls and I guarantee you'll find yourself running . . .'

'. . . running for the loo,' Joe thought to himself and went on his way.

In the next twenty minutes, he covered the entire hotel and came to two inescapable conclusions.

The Stilton International had been built by grannies, for grannies and was run by grannies.

And everyone who came there

wanted to be young again. They were obsessed with it.

So where, he wondered, did that leave him?

The thought was still on his mind as he joined Granny for dinner. This was served in a large room with ten round tables, each seating eight or nine grannies. Joe was joined by the four grannies he recognized from the card game at Thattlebee Hall—Granny Anne, Granny Smith, Granny Adams and Granny Lee—as well as two other grannies he didn't know. None of them spoke to him although Granny Adams spent several minutes examining him through her inch-thick spectacles until the first course was served.

The first course was quail's eggs. The grannies fell on them like wolves.

Joe remembered an old phrase he had once heard. 'You can't teach Grandma to suck eggs.' He could certainly see it was true now as the ninety grannies in the room grabbed the miniature eggs, smashed the shells against their plates, the tables or indeed each other and then sucked out the contents. Soon the whole room was filled with the sound of slurping as the balls of glistening white were vacuumed. Granny Smith—the fat granny—was enjoying hers so much that she wasn't even bothering to remove the shells. Joe wondered if there might be a prize for the granny who sucked the most eggs, and that made him think of the Golden Granny Awards he had seen advertised.

He turned to Granny. 'What are the Golden Granny Awards?' he asked.

Granny looked at him suspiciously. 'Never you mind,' she snapped. 'They've got nothing to do with you.'

'Past your bedtime,' Granny Smith added, picking a piece of eggshell out of her teeth.

'When is his bedtime?' Granny Lee asked.

Granny looked at her watch. 'Now!'

'But . . .' Joe began. He glanced at the kitchen door, which had just opened. A waiter was carrying in a vast silver dish of poached eels with mashed potato. Joe blinked. 'Maybe you're right,' he said. 'I am a bit tired.'

Joe got up and left the room. As he went he felt himself being followed by a hundred and eighty eyes (three of them glass). He saw one granny nudge another and point, heard a soft chuckle as his name was whispered. 'Jordan . . . that's the boy . . . Ivy Kettle's boy . . .'

The first eels were being served as he left. Netted, boiled and stretched out on a plate . . . Joe knew exactly how they felt.

*   *   *

Of course, he didn't go to sleep.

At ten o'clock exactly he crept back downstairs, avoiding the lift in case the noise gave him away. The hotel was in half-darkness, the front doors locked, the reception area empty. The receptionist was still behind the desk, but she had fallen asleep.

10.00 p.m. The Elsie Bucket Conference Room . . .

Although Joe hadn't been inside the room on his tour of the hotel, he found it easily enough, following the sign out of the reception area and past the health food shop. As he padded along the thickly carpeted corridor towards a pair of heavy wooden doors, he heard a woman's voice, amplified by a microphone system but still muffled by the wall.

'And welcome, ladies and ladies, to the annual Golden Granny Awards . . .'

There was a round of applause.

Taking his courage—and the handles—in both hands, Joe opened the doors and quickly stepped inside. He would never forget the sight that met his eyes.

The Elsie Bucket Conference Room was enormous. It was a long, low-ceilinged room with a wooden floor and a stage at the far end. It had seats for about two hundred and fifty people and every one was taken. Joe realized that as well as the grannies in the hotel other grannies must have travelled from all over the country to be here. There were grannies in every seat—two to a seat in places. There were more grannies standing at the sides and yet more grannies hunched up on the floor in front of the stage.

The stage itself was decorated with a rippling wall of gold in front of which hung a sign: THE GOLDEN GRANNY AWARDS. The awards themselves—little statuettes of golden tortoises—were arranged on a nearby table. There was a granny sitting at a piano whilst an elderly man addressed the audience. Joe thought he recognized him as someone who had once done magic tricks or something on television—but that had been about five years ago. His name was Dan Parnell and he was wearing a red dinner jacket and a silver bow tie.

Joe had entered the room at the very back. He slid behind a row of spotlights and watched with bated breath.

'As you know,' Dan Parnell said, 'every year we give out these awards to the grannies who have most distinguished themselves in certain fields.'

'I've never been in a field!' someone shouted from the back and all the other grannies screeched with laughter.

'The tortoise lives for many, many years,' the man went on. 'And this is why our awards take the form of a tortoise. Do you know, ladies, that the combined ages of everyone in this room add up to twenty-two thousand, five hundred!'

This news was greeted by a huge round of applause, cat-calls and stamping feet. Joe watched nervously as the spotlights trembled and shook. Dan Parnell held up a hand for silence.

'Nobody wants to be old,' he went on. 'Let's face it! Being old is beastly. And it's not just the wrinkles and the false teeth.' He pulled open his mouth to show his own which glinted in the light. 'It's not just the aches and the nasal hair. What hurts is having to stand by and watch young people take over. That's what I hate. That's what we all hate.'

There was another explosion of applause which went on a full ten minutes.

'But we can have our revenge!' Dan Parnell continued at last. 'We can get in their way. We can upset them. We can do all sorts of things if we set our minds to it—and we can have a lot of fun. That's what these awards are about and without any more ado, let's get on with the presentation.'

Joe peered out as Dan Parnell went over to the row of tortoises. The granny at the piano played a few dramatic chords. The grannies in the audience clapped and punched at the air with clenched fists.

'The first award is for the longest time getting on a bus. This award has been won this year by Rita Sponge who managed to take a staggering three-quarters of an hour getting on a 19 bus at Piccadilly Circus!' There was a burst of applause, but Dan held up a hand for silence. 'And—wait for it—she then managed to spend another twenty-three minutes looking for her bus pass! An amazing one hour eight minutes in total!'

This time the applause was loud and sustained as Granny Sponge—a tall, drooping woman with wet, red eyes—came onto the stage to collect her award.

'The second award is for the longest queue in a post office. Again, another record, ladies and ladies. Forty-five people kept waiting for over half an hour in the Bath post office. And the man behind her actually had a nervous breakdown! Step forward Doreen Beavis!'

Granny Beavis was small and lively. She was so excited by her award that, having snatched it, she actually fell off the stage. But this only delighted the other grannies all the more.

'And now we come to the Elsie Bucket Difficult Shopper award. A very close result this year. Congratulations to Enid Crabb who spent the whole day in Harrods and had every single video recorder demonstrated to her three times without actually buying one. Also congratulations to Betty Brush for buying half an ounce of every single meat on display at her local supermarket, a performance that took three hours and kept sixty-one people waiting. But I'm afraid you were both pipped to the post by this year's winner, Nora Strapp, who spent so long complaining about a Biro she had bought at Woolworth's that the manager eventually committed suicide. Well done, Nora!'

Everyone applauded (apart from Enid Crabb and Betty Brush). Nora Strapp picked up her award and pranced off the stage.

Joe watched, unbelieving, as the other awards were presented. There was an award for the most unnecessary visits to a doctor and an award for the most absurd reason for telephoning the police. One granny picked up an award for causing the worst scene at a wedding, whilst another was unable to pick up her award for causing the most violent argument in a family as she was still in hospital.

Joe's granny didn't win anything but Granny Smith got an honourable mention for the most damage caused when trying to be helpful.

An hour later, the last award had been given and Dan Parnell had left the room to huge applause. Joe was just preparing to sneak back to his bedroom when another granny took the stage. She was older than anyone in the room. Looking at her, at the hundreds of wrinkles on her face, at the white hair reaching down to her shoulders and her trembling, claw-like hands, Joe would have said she was well over a hundred. There were terrible blotches on her cheeks. Her eyes were completely empty.

'And now . . .' she screeched—she had a terrible, sandpaper voice—'the moment we have all been waiting for! But before I go on, I must introduce our uninvited guest!'

Our uninvited guest . . .

Somehow Joe knew who the old woman was talking about and he went hot and cold at exactly the same time. She was gazing at him now, her eyes as welcoming as a shark's. He took one step back.

A huge net fell over his head, reaching down all the way to his feet. He looked up and realized that there was a balcony running along the back of the hall, that there were another ten grannies up there and that he had been observed from the moment he had come in. It had been they who had

126

dropped the net. Now another four grannies ran forward and seized the corners. He tried to struggle but it was hopeless. He had been netted like a north Atlantic cod.

Joe squirmed and kicked, only entangling himself all the more. Somewhere in his mind he swore never to eat another fish-finger. But it was too late for that.

'Bring him forward!' the old woman cried. With the cackling of the grannies all around him, Joe was dragged onto the stage.

THE GRANNYMATIC
ENZYME EXTRACTOR

'You all know me,' the oldest granny exclaimed.

Joe was on the stage beside her, struggling and straining. The grannies had not only tied him up—that would have been bad enough. They had also fastened him into a strait-jacket which they had evidently knitted themselves as it was made out of pink wool.

'My name is Elsie Bucket,' the woman went on, 'and I am the oldest granny in Great Britain. One hundred and six years old today!'

There was loud applause from the audience but Elsie Bucket did not smile. She held up a grey, skeletal hand for silence.

'Yes,' she said. 'I have received seven telegrams from the Queen. Seven telegrams! But have I so much as received one single present? Not on your nelly!' She sniffed. 'So much for

128

the Queen!'

She walked slowly to the front of the stage.

'I am old and like you, fellow grannies, I do not wish to be old. All my life I have thought about this. I was so afraid of being old that I never actually enjoyed being young. Fortunately, however, I was a brilliant scientist. It was I, for example, who invented the telephone. I can't tell you how angry I was when my sister rang me to tell me it had already been invented. Even so, I managed to invent the telephone bill. From there I went on to invent the electricity meter, the television licence and, later, the wheel-clamp.

'However, my greatest invention has taken me sixty years. It is here tonight. You, dear grannies, have all brought with you one component—as I asked you to in this very room last year. What a wonderful achievement! From a simple light bulb to an electro-static de-energizer, from a long-life battery to a teaspoon of nuclear fuel, you have all brought exactly what I asked of you.

But here I must say a special "thank you" to Ivy Kettle.' Joe stopped struggling and glowered at his granny who was sitting in the third row with a smug look on her face. Elsie Bucket gestured at her. 'It was Ivy who provided us with the single most important—and potentially the most difficult—component of all. He may be small and rather unhygienic. But he's real. He's alive (for the time being). And he's here. She brought us a boy!'

'A boy! Oh joy! A boy!'

The grannies had all gone into ecstasies like very religious people at a prayer meeting. Joe felt the blood rush into his face as they all gazed at him, screeching and clapping, pointing and grinning. One granny had become so excited that she had gone red in the face and keeled over in her chair—but everyone ignored her in the general chaos. Joe was certain that at any moment he would wake up in bed. It was all a nightmare. It had to be. To be tied up in a pink strait-jacket in a Devonshire hotel with over five hundred grannies hooting at you—that sort of thing just couldn't possibly happen in the real world.

Except that it had. This was no dream.

'And so, fellow grannies, no more talk! No more waiting! Let us do what we have so looked forward to doing. And let me show you my invention. Grannies—I give you . . . the Grannymatic Enzyme Extractor!'

There was a hush in the room as the gold curtain slid back and even Joe gasped when he saw what had been constructed there at the back of the stage.

At first he thought it was an electric chair. An ordinary wooden chair was indeed part of it with coils and wires twisting round the legs and vanishing under the seat. But there was much more to it than that. A maze of glass pipes and tubes zigzagged and spiralled away into a line of bottles, some of them empty, some of them filled with a dark green liquid. A circular gauge reading 'EMPTY' in blue and 'FULL' in red hung from a tangle of wires with a golden arrow waiting to travel the distance between the two. The object that looked like a glass and steel tuba—Joe had seen it briefly in the reception area—was now suspended above the machine. Joe realized it could be lowered onto the head of whoever sat there. It in turn was connected to a complicated metal structure surrounding the chair and— Joe swallowed hard when he saw this— there were no fewer than thirteen large hypodermic syringes pointing inwards, attached to it at different levels. Joe imagined himself sitting in the chair (somehow it wasn't very hard to do) and saw that there would be two needles pointing at his ankles, two at his knees, two at his thighs, one at his stomach, one at the small of his back, two at his elbows, two at his neck and one—the highest—at the centre of his forehead. The syringes, big enough to inject a horse, were built into gold, magnetic coils. All of them were wired up to work automatically.

The whole ghastly contraption was connected to a control desk a few feet away. This was made up of the usual array of dials and gauges, flashing lights and buttons that he had seen on every episode of *Star Trek*. The only difference was that it had also been decorated with a small lace cloth and a flower in a pot. There was a comfy armchair behind it for the operator to sit on.

'Take him!' Elsie Bucket commanded.

Joe lashed out as the four grannies who had captured him fell on him again, giggling and wheezing. But he was helpless. As old and as weak as they were there were four of them and he was pinioned by the strait-jacket. They pulled him, dragging his heels across the stage, and tied him into the chair. Two leather straps went over his legs, two more across his chest, one on each arm and a final one around his throat. There was nothing he could do.

He sat, facing the audience, half-blinded by the spotlights that were trained on him. He could just make out the small round heads staring at him like so many coconuts behind the glare but he was aware only of the thirteen needles pointing towards him. His hand grappled for a wire or a circuit he could pull . . . anything to sabotage the machine. But he had been tied too tightly and the chair had been too well designed. Gritting his teeth, he slumped back. Now he could only wait.

'The Grannymatic Enzyme Extractor!' Elsie Bucket announced, moving into the light. 'Last year, you will recall, we tested my elixir of life, the secret potion that would make me and all my dear granny friends young again. Over one hundred ingredients had gone into my elixir of life! Avocado oil, ginseng, yoghurt, royal jelly, raw oysters, ox blood, iron oxide, zinc, milk of magnesia, yak's milk, cactus juice, the yolk of an ostrich egg and much, much more. But it didn't work. And why didn't it work? Because there was one missing ingredient.

'Enzymes are the stuff of life. Without enzymes there can be no life. And this boy's enzymes, added to my wonderful elixir, will turn back the clock and instantly return us to our glorious, wonderful youth! And what about this glorious, wonderful youth?' Elsie Bucket pointed at Joe. 'Sadly, the operation will kill the child. But I am sure even he won't mind when he knows how happy he will be making all of us.'

'I do mind!' Joe shouted.

Elsie Bucket ignored him. 'In a minute I shall flick the switch,' she said. 'The machine will do the rest. His enzymes will be sucked out of him. They will travel down these pipes here . . .' She pointed them out. 'They will be thoroughly disinfected and then added to my elixir here.' She tapped on one of the jars of green liquid. 'From just one boy I estimate we can make five hundred doses, enough for everyone here! By the time the process is over,' she added almost as an afterthought, 'the boy will be as shrivelled as an overcooked cocktail sausage. If you find this disturbing, I suggest you don't look.'

'I find it disturbing!' Joe cried out. But Elsie Bucket was already leaning over him, lowering the tuba-contraption onto his head. 'A little electro-massage,' she whispered to him. 'Very painful, but it helps the enzymes flow.'

'You're mad!' Joe spat out the words.

'How dare you talk to an old lady like that!' Elsie Bucket smiled, her face close to his, and Joe saw her grey tongue loll out of her mouth like a dying slug, then curl back to lick her ancient, discoloured teeth and suddenly he was more sick than afraid.

'Now!' Elsie Bucket sang out the word.

'Now!' the grannies chorused.

'No!' Joe strained with every muscle but the straps that held him were too thick.

Elsie Bucket capered over to the control desk and sat down in the armchair. She raised her hands and flexed her fingers as if she were a concert pianist. Joe heard the bones clicking against each other.

Then she stabbed down.

The machine hummed and whirred into life. The green liquid bubbled. The light bulbs blinked and flickered.

The leather straps around him seemed to tighten but perhaps that was his own body tensing up as it all began. Electricity buzzed through the tuba-helmet which began to grow hot against his head. Joe clawed at the arms of the chair as slowly, one after another, the hypodermic needles shivered and then began to move forward. The arrow on the EMPTY and FULL gauge trembled excitedly. The whole thing was rattling and shaking, as indeed were all the watching grannies.

The hypodermic syringes slid forward.

Elsie Bucket yanked at a lever, her eyes bulging, her whole face twitching with delight.

The green liquid in the bottles surged and boiled. Electricity flickered. The needles moved again.

Joe opened his mouth to scream.

And then all the lights went out and everything stopped.

For a long moment nobody did anything. Then Joe heard Elsie Bucket's voice calling out of the darkness. 'Don't panic, grannies! It's only a fuse. We'll have it mended in a moment!'

But even as she spoke, Joe was aware of someone close by him. He felt warm breath on his cheek. A pair of hands reached out to undo first the strap around his throat, then the ones on his arms. And at the same time a voice spoke to him. It was a voice he recognized, a woman's. But he still couldn't see.

'Run for it, Joe,' the voice whispered. 'Get out of here and get back to London. You can do it!'

The remaining straps fell away. The knitted strait-jacket was cut through with a single stroke. There was a pause and Joe realized that his mysterious rescuer had gone and that he was once more on his own. He stood up.

The lights came back on. The Grannymatic Enzyme Extractor shuddered back into life.

Elsie Bucket stood inches away, staring at him, her face twisted with fury. 'Stop him!' she screamed in a voice that could have broken glass.

'He's getting away!' At the same time she reached out to grab Joe herself.

Joe did the only thing he could. He twisted to one side and pushed Elsie Bucket away. Elsie gave a small, despairing gurgle and fell backwards into the seat of the Extractor just as the thirteen needles jerked forward like angry snakes. Joe didn't see what happened next. He was already running towards the edge of the stage, searching for a way out. But he heard Elsie Bucket's final scream as she was thoroughly punctured. He heard the great wail from the grannies in the audience. And he heard the sucking and bubbling as the Grannymatic Enzyme Extractor did what it had been built for.

Elsie Bucket had received her last royal telegram. The machine had attempted to extract her enzymes but having failed to find any had extracted everything else. There was nothing left of the granny apart from her clothes, punctured in thirteen places. These were now draped over the wooden seat with a few wisps of black smoke curling upwards into the light. At the same time a horrible grey ooze travelled along the tangle of pipes and spat itself out into the waiting bottles.

In the audience, the grannies moaned, yelled and bit each other, uncertain what to do next. The machine had finished with Elsie Bucket and was now vibrating dangerously, trying to tear free of the stage. A few yards away, Joe found a fire exit and, taking a deep breath, reached for the handle. He felt the cold steel under his hand and pushed. Mercifully, the door was unlocked. He felt the handle give and the door open and then he was out, tumbling into the night air.

And at that precise moment, the Grannymatic Enzyme Extractor exploded. Joe felt a fist of hot air punch him in the back. He was thrown forward, somersaulting twice and landing in a bed of flowers. He tried to stand up, then winced and covered his head as bricks, tiles, windows, wigs and false teeth showered down all around him. It seemed to go on for ever but at last everything was silent again and slowly, painfully, he got up.

The Stilton International had been partially destroyed. There was nothing left of the Elsie Bucket Conference Room. Nor could he make out a single surviving granny. It was like pictures he had seen of the Second World War—jagged broken walls, thick smoke, fires burning in the wreckage. Already the fire brigade and ambulance service had been alerted. He could hear their sirens in the far distance.

And then somebody moved, limping painfully through the smoke, coughing and spluttering. Joe tried to run but he had sprained his ankle and he could only wait there as the figure approached.

It was Granny.

Somehow Joe wasn't surprised that she had survived. But the explosion had not left her unharmed. She had lost a large clump of her hair and all her remaining teeth. Her arms and legs were covered in cuts and bruises and her twenty-seven-year-old coat hung off her in ribbons.

The two of them stood gazing at

each other in the debris. At last Granny spoke.

'Are you all right, Jamie, my dear?'

'My name is Joe—and I'm not your dear!'

'Oh, yes you are.' Granny's eyes flickered over to what had been the Elsie Bucket Suite. 'We're very lucky,' she said. 'We seem to be the only survivors of an unfortunate accident . . .'

'An accident?'

'Oh, yes. It must have been the gas. Of course, that's what it was. Somebody must have left the oven on.'

'I'm going to tell the truth!' Joe snarled.

Granny just smiled. 'You could try telling your version of the truth, but do you really think anyone would believe you? A twelve-year-old boy? They'd think you were mad, Jeffrey. They'd lock you up.'

Joe glanced at the wreckage of the hotel and realized that she was right. There would be nothing left of the Grannymatic Enzyme Extractor—and even if they managed to find a few tubes and valves, what expert would be able to work out what they were really for? Even as he watched, the flames leaped up, finding a way through the bricks and rubble.

Granny took a step nearer. Joe stood his ground. 'Maybe you're right,' he said. 'But you can't hurt me any more. I know about you. And one day . . .'

'One day what?' Joe had been too kind, even now, to say what he was thinking. But now Granny said it for him. 'One day I'll be dead? Is that what you're thinking?' She smiled toothlessly in the moonlight. Smoke from the ruined building curled around her legs. 'Oh, yes. Even I won't live for ever. But don't you see, Joe, you'll never be rid of me. Because, you see, when I die, I'll come back. I'll come back and haunt you and there's nothing you'll be able to do.'

'You're lying,' Joe whispered. The fire engines were getting nearer. He could hear the engines now, racing up the hill.

'Oh, no! The grave won't keep me lying down for long. I'll come back,

you'll see. Just when you least expect it
. . .' Her eyes blinked, black in the
white light of the moon. 'And then . . .
oh yes, what fun we'll have.'

Half a minute later the firemen
arrived with the police right behind
them. They found one old lady waiting
for them in the garden. She was
standing next to a twelve-year-old boy
lying flat out on the grass.

'You'd better look after my
grandson,' she said in a feeble, tearful
voice as they wrapped a blanket round
her and led her away. 'He seems to
have fainted. I suppose it must have
been the shock.'

GOODBYE, GRANNY

Mr and Mrs Warden returned from the south of France a few days later. They had not had a good holiday. Mr Warden had fallen asleep in the sun and was horribly burned. The top of his bald head was a glowing red and three layers of skin had peeled off his nose. He couldn't sit down without crying. Mrs Warden had been bitten by three hundred mosquitoes. Attracted by her body spray, they had invaded her bed and bitten every inch from her ankles to her ears. Her face in particular was dreadfully swollen. When Mr Warden had woken up beside her the following morning, he had actually screamed.

Wolfgang and Irma returned from Hungary the day after. They enjoyed their holiday so much that in the four weeks they had been away they had forgotten how to speak

English. They had brought everyone souvenirs of Hungary: a beetroot for Mr Warden, a book of Hungarian poetry for Mrs Warden and furry hats for Joe and Granny.

As for Granny herself, Joe had seen little of her after the events in Bideford. They had been released from hospital after one night's surveillance and had travelled back to London on the first train. The police had asked them a lot of questions but both of them had pretended they were asleep when the hotel exploded. Joe had hated doing it but he knew he had no choice. He was only twelve. Nobody would have believed him.

Even so, he got grim amusement from reading the newspapers the following day. He had always suspected you couldn't believe half the things you read in the papers but now he knew it was all a pack of lies.

300 GRANNIES PERISH
IN HOTEL HORROR
FAULTY FUSE BLAMED FOR
BIDEFORD BANG
BRITAIN GRIEVES FOR
GRANNIES
QUEEN MUM SENDS MESSAGE

He had stayed with Granny at Thattlebee Hall for five days but in that time he had barely seen her. When his parents got home, she had left without saying goodbye.

However, she had managed to play one last mean trick on him.

On Sunday, a new nanny arrived. Apparently Granny had interviewed and selected her personally before she had gone. The new nanny was a short, plain woman wearing no make-up and a dress that seemed to have been fashioned out of a potato sack. Her hair was grey, as indeed was the rest of her. Her name, she said, was Ms Whipsnade.

'Miss Whipsnade,' Wolfgang announced as he opened the door to her.

'I said Ms,' the new nanny exclaimed, dropping her suitcase on Wolfgang's foot.

It turned out that Ms Whipsnade had worked for sixteen years as a social worker before going into politics. She was a communist and had stood for Parliament seven times. At the last election she had got four votes against the winner's twenty-six thousand, five hundred and eighty. Even so, she had demanded a recount. Ms Whipsnade was also a strict vegetarian and actually wept when she saw Joe's leather shoes. Neither Mr Warden nor his wife were entirely sure about the new arrival but as Granny had already offered her the job, there wasn't much they could do. And so Ms Whipsnade was shown to her room—which she promptly declared a nuclear-free zone. She also tore off all the wallpaper in the mistaken belief that it had been printed in South Africa.

On the following Monday, much to his relief, Joe went back to school. He had hardly slept at all since that night in Bideford and there were dark rings around his eyes. It wasn't just the horror of the Grannymatic Enzyme Extractor. That had almost faded in his mind. Much, much worse was his last encounter with Granny, outside in the wreckage. Her words seemed to hang like cobwebs in the darkness and her beady eyes and twisted mouth were somehow always there—just out of sight. He realized now that he was more afraid of Granny dead than he was of her alive.

And that of course was exactly what she had intended. Alone in his room, Joe counted the hours until daylight and the days until he would be back at school. There at least he would be surrounded by young, happy, normal people. He felt safer with other children. Other children were all right. Anybody old—the headmaster, the dinner lady, the caretaker, the lollipop lady—now belonged to another, twilight world. Joe looked at them and he was afraid.

Time passed and for a while everything was all right.

Then Granny fell ill.

Joe first heard the news one afternoon at school. After lunch he was called into the headmaster's study. The headmaster, a white-haired man of about sixty, was called Mr Ellis. He had been a teacher for forty-four years even though he was allergic to children. He was sitting in a large leather chair when Joe came in. 'Do sit down, Warden,' he said. 'Sit down.'

That was when Joe knew it had to be bad news.

Mr Ellis sneezed. 'I'm afraid I have some bad news for you, Warden. It's your grandmother . . .'

'She's not dead, is she?' Joe exclaimed.

'No! No!' The headmaster was surprised by the boy's alarm. He sneezed twice more and tried to shrink into his chair. 'No. But it is quite serious. Pneumonia.'

'She can't die!' Joe whispered. 'She can't!'

Mr Ellis blinked. 'I have to say, it's rare to find a boy so fond of his granny,' he muttered. He pulled out a handkerchief and dabbed at his eye. 'It does you credit, Warden. I'm sure she'll be all right. But in the meantime, perhaps it would be better if you went home.'

Joe returned home that afternoon. The new nanny was in his room, painting pink triangles on his walls to show her support for the gay movement. She had also donated his bed and all his books to the Cuban miners.

'How's Granny?' Joe asked.

Ms Whipsnade blinked. 'Her name is Ms Kettle,' she snapped. 'As a term, "granny" is both sexist and, worse, ageist.'

'How is she?'

'I haven't heard. For some reason your parents refuse to speak to me.'

For the next few days there were a lot of comings and goings at Thattlebee Hall. Car doors slammed at all times of the day and night and Mr and Mrs Warden seemed to speak permanently in whispers. Nobody told Joe anything and the first inkling he had that things were really serious was when he saw his Uncles David and Kurt arrive at the front door. The relations never came to the house unless it was for Christmas or a funeral and Christmas had been over long ago. Listening at the door, Joe learned that Granny's pneumonia had got worse and that her doctors had more or less given up hope. His uncles were already arguing about her will.

And then on Friday morning came the news. Granny had died in her sleep.

At breakfast, Wolfgang and Irma were both tearful. Meanwhile, Ms Whipsnade—imitating the burial customs of the Taramuhara Indians—danced in the garden and set fire to the summer house. Later that morning, as soon as the fire brigade had gone, Mrs Warden went to Harrods and bought herself a black Yves St Laurent dress with a crepe tunic, silk veil and diamante trim. Mr Warden spent most of the time on the telephone. He then drank an entire bottle of champagne. Irma assumed he was drowning his sorrows but Joe wasn't so sure. Certainly his father was singing merrily enough when he was carried to bed.

The funeral took place on the Sunday. It was a terrible day. The weather had turned and the various relatives—the Wardens and the Kettles—had to battle their way into the cemetery against the howling wind and rain. It seemed that the entire family had turned out: Michael, David, Kurt and Nita were there along with Joe's four cousins (all in black shorts—the rainwater streaming in rivulets down their legs). But there were other relatives too: tiny Aunt Cissie, fat cousin Sidney and twitching Uncle Geoff. Then there was Uncle Fred who had flown all the way from Texas to be there and several other relatives whom Joe didn't recognize.

Wisely, the vicar kept the sermon short. The weather was just too horrible. After two minutes, Aunt Cissie was actually blown into the open grave by a particularly vicious gust of wind. The rain lashed down and all the colour ran out of Uncle Fred's suit— soon he was standing in a puddle of blue ink. About halfway through the service there was a great flash of lightning and Uncle David had an epileptic fit. The four cousins left early with chilblains. Even the vicar looked alarmed and managed to get most of the words wrong. All in all it was a dreadful affair.

But worse, in some ways, were the days that followed. Joe had been left out of everything—as if he were too young to understand funerals, deaths and the rest of it. As for Ms Whipsnade, she had been fired after she had told Mrs Warden that her mother had not died so much as been recycled. A great silence had descended on Thattlebee Hall. It wasn't that the house was in mourning. That would have been perfectly understandable. No. It was something altogether different and more difficult to explain.

For his part, Joe was terrified.

'I'll come back . . .'

What could he do? He couldn't sleep. He couldn't even relax. He had lost so much weight that he had to look twice to find himself in the mirror. At any time he expected to see Granny

154

return. How would it happen? Would she dig her way out of the grave and return, dripping mud and slime, to the house? Or would she come in the night, materializing suddenly above his bed and floating around the room? Not for a minute did he doubt that Granny would return. She had promised it and he had seen the certainty in her eyes.

Inevitably, Joe himself fell ill. His temperature shot up to one hundred and three and the sweat poured off him as he tossed and turned in his bed. He hadn't eaten anything for a week and his ribs were so pronounced that Wolfgang—much to everyone's amazement—was able to use them to demonstrate his skill as a xylophone player. Doctors were called in and, after listening to Joe's feverish cries, announced that he had been traumatized by his granny's death. It seemed more than likely that he was about to join her.

Joe did have moments when he was cool and rational. It was at these times that he tried to work out what to do. He knew he was afraid—that he was actually being scared to death by the memory of what Granny had said. And he also knew he had to tell someone about it. That was the only way to bring the nightmare to an end. Tell someone and they'd be able to face it together. But at the same time he knew there was no one. He couldn't go to his parents. Mrs Jinks and Mr Lampy were both gone. He was on his own.

And then the postcard came.

It was addressed to him, written in neat, block capitals. On the front was a picture of Bideford. On the back was a simple message:

THE TRUTH WILL ALWAYS COME OUT.

That was all. The card was unsigned.

Joe thought long and hard. He knew he had heard the words before but he couldn't remember where. The only clue seemed to be the picture of Bideford. He had often wondered who it was who had freed him from the Enzyme Extractor while the lights were out, and had played the voice in his mind over and over again. He had always assumed that it must have been one of the grannies who had taken pity on him and who had perished in the blast. But now, looking at the card, he wasn't so sure. 'The truth will always come out.' Who had said that to him and when?

From that time on, Joe began to recover. It wasn't just the fact that he knew that, after all, he did have a friend. It was also his belief in what the postcard said. The truth was important. The truth mattered. It mattered more than the fact that he was only twelve and that his story was completely preposterous. People like Granny, all bullies in fact, only managed to survive because they lived behind the truth. Once people knew them for what they were, they would be powerless.

One evening, a week after the funeral, Joe got out of bed and went downstairs. His parents were in the sitting-room, watching television. It was *The Money Programme*, his father's favourite, but even so he pressed ahead.

Joe told them.

He turned off the television and told

them everything that had happened since Christmas and the toy robot. He told them about the cream cheese tea, the death of Mrs Jinks and his suspicions about the death of Mr Lampy. Then he told them what had really happened in Bideford, what had caused the explosion and how he had escaped.

Mr and Mrs Warden listened to all this in complete silence but when he had at last finished, Mrs Warden stood up.

'Is that all?' she asked.

'Yes,' Joe said. He cast his eyes down. The room was suddenly like a refrigerator. He could feel his mother's anger, chilling him.

'You do realize that's my mother you're talking about?'

'Yes.'

Mrs Warden let out a single sob. 'We'll discuss this in the morning,' she said and walked out of the room with her nose in the air.

'Look where you're going!' Mr Warden shouted.

There was a loud clunk as Mrs

Warden hit the corner of the door. Then she was gone.

'Now look what you've done,' Mr Warden snapped. He did the same to his cigar even though it was only half-smoked. 'Lost your marbles, have you?' he asked.

'Father . . .'

'I've heard some pretty daft stories in my time,' he said. 'But that one takes the biscuit. And on the subject of biscuits it's time for my hot milk. I'll talk to you in the morning, young man!'

Joe watched his father leave. For the first time in more years than he could remember he felt hot tears brimming on his eyelids. 'I hate this house,' he muttered. 'I hate them all.' He was still holding the mysterious postcard. Now he tore it into pieces. He didn't care who had sent it any more. Nobody would ever believe him. Nobody cared about him. He was nobody.

That was the truth.

* * *

Later that evening, Mr and Mrs

Warden lay in bed. Mr Warden had decided against the hot milk and was sipping a glass of brandy instead. Mrs Warden was half-concealed under an ice-pack which was pressed against her face where the door had hit her.

'That story,' Mr Warden muttered. 'It was ridiculous.'

'Ludicrous,' Mrs Warden agreed.

'Outrageous.'

'Monstrous.'

'Your mother . . . she would never have behaved like that!'

'Of course not!'

'No.'

There was a long silence.

'She was rather horrible to me once or twice, though,' Mr Warden murmured. 'Of course, I adored her. She was your mother. But she could be . . . difficult.'

'I suppose so,' Mrs Warden agreed.

'I mean, she never liked me,' Mr Warden went on. 'When I asked if I could marry you, she poured tea over me. And her wedding present to us. Twelve fish-fingers. That wasn't very generous.'

'She could be worse,' Mrs Warden murmured. 'When I was a little girl, she made me share my room with two lodgers, one of whom—Mr Baster— had very unsavoury habits. And do you know, she never took me out once. Not in my whole life!'

'Really?' Mr Warden was genuinely surprised.

'Not even shopping. She never had any time for me. She once told me she didn't want children. She'd even tried to abandon me. She left me in a basket on the steps of a police station.'

'Good lord! How distressing.'

'It was very embarrassing. I was sixteen years old!'

Mr Warden reflected. 'Your father adored her, though,' he said.

'Yes. He did adore her. Only he forgot their anniversary once and she never spoke to him again.'

'She was a hard woman.'

'Oh, yes.'

Both of them sat in silence again. Then Mr Warden scooped a cube out of his wife's ice-pack and added it to his brandy. 'I suppose Jordan's story could be true, then,' he muttered.

'Yes. I suppose so.'

'I mean, she was a hard woman.'

'Very hard.'

On the mantelpiece, the clock struck ten although in fact it was half past nine. The clock had never worked properly since Granny, in a moment of anger, had stamped on it.

'Of course,' he went on, 'it's very sad, your mother passing away like that.'

'It's devastating,' Mrs Warden agreed.

'Tragic.'

'Terrible.'

'Too, too awful! I'll miss her . . .' Mr Warden took a large gulp of brandy.

'Will you?' Mrs Warden asked.

'Well, I will a bit.' Mr Warden swallowed. 'But to tell you the truth, my love, I wasn't a hundred per cent fond of her.'

'Not a hundred per cent?'

'No.'

'Fifty perhaps?'

'Well . . . not even fifty.' Mr Warden frowned. 'I know it's a horrible thing to say, my angel. But no. If you really

162

want the truth, I wasn't very fond of her at all.'

Mrs Warden slid the ice-pack off her head. Most of it had melted now anyway. 'Nor was I,' she whispered.

'What?'

'Oh, Gordon! It's dreadful of me. She was my mother. But I have to admit it. It's true. I really didn't love her.'

'I never looked forward to her visits,' Mr Warden said.

'I dreaded them.'

'I hated them!'

'I loathed them!'

Mr and Mrs Warden looked at each other. And in that moment—perhaps the first true moment they had shared together in twenty years of marriage—they understood many things.

The first was that they had lied to each other. The second was that they had lied to themselves. That was what was so odd and uncomfortable about this period of mourning. They weren't really mourning at all. They weren't glad that old Mrs Kettle was dead. They would never have thought that about anyone. But they couldn't honestly say that they would miss her—which was what they had been saying. That was all a lie.

Their marriage was full of lies too. They could see that now, sitting in bed with Mrs Warden's ice-pack dripping onto the electric blanket. And without saying anything they knew they had come to a crossroads. Mrs Warden was beginning to wonder if perhaps, just possibly, she hadn't treated her only child just a little bit like her mother had always treated her. And Mr Warden too was asking himself what sort of father he had really been. For that matter, what sort of husband had he been? What sort of man was he? Everything had been poisoned by lies.

And then both Mr and Mrs Warden had the same thought at the same time.

'That business about her . . . coming back,' Mr Warden said.

'She won't,' Mrs Warden muttered. 'I mean, let's be adult about this, Gordon, dearest. It's not possible.'

'It's absurd.'

'Nonsensical.'

'Out of the question.'

Mr and Mrs Warden edged closer to each other in bed. Mr Warden put his arms around Mrs Warden. Mrs Warden put her arms around Mr Warden. There was a sudden fizz, a flash and all the lights in the house went out as the electric blanket short-circuited. The two parents were plunged into blackness.

'She won't come back,' Mr Warden's voice quavered in the dark. 'She can't . . .'

But they were still clinging onto each other when dawn finally broke and the first fingers of light announced the next day.

GRANNY COMES BACK

Curiously, Granny wasn't actually dead. This is what had happened.

She had indeed been taken ill with a bad cold and, before she had even sneezed twice, she had telephoned for an ambulance to take her to hospital. By the time the ambulance men had arrived, she had decided she was too ill even to walk and had insisted on being carried to the waiting vehicle. It was then that something very unfortunate had taken place.

As the ambulance men carried her out of the block of flats a neighbour had chanced to walk past and asked them if they knew the time. Both ambulance men had lifted their wrists to look at their watches. In doing so, they unwittingly tilted the stretcher. This was a bad mistake. Granny gave a little scream and rolled off the stretcher, falling straight into a large puddle. The result was that by the time she arrived at the hospital, Granny's cold really had developed into a mild form of pneumonia and she had to be given a bed.

Even so, her illness was not life-threatening. The doctors were sure she would be able to go home in a day or two and left her quite happily sitting up in bed with a furry knitted jacket and the latest copy of *Hello!* magazine.

Now, Granny had been placed in an ordinary public ward—in the geriatric wing. There were eight beds there and each one was occupied . . . indeed one bed actually had two elderly people in it, lying head-to-foot and foot-to-head—as ever, the National Health Service was finding it hard to cope. But despite the crowding, the nurses and doctors were as cheerful as possible, working long hours into the night, and nobody complained.

Nobody, that is, except for the woman in the bed next to Granny.

Her name was Marjory Henslow and she was a retired headmistress. Having spent her whole working life telling people what to do, she hadn't allowed retirement to stop her. She treated the nurses, the cleaners and her fellow patients like children, her face frozen in a permanent sneer of disapproval. She was a woman with opinions about everything and expressed them at all times of the day and night.

'Mrs Thatcher? A wonderful woman! She showed them in the Gulf War. That's what the train drivers need. A few Exocet missiles would soon show them what's what! I'd blow them all up. And the miners! I say we should close all the pits down. What's wrong with nuclear energy? Let's drop nuclear bombs on the miners and the teachers and the train drivers. Bing! Bang! Boom! When I was a headmistress I used to flog everyone. It never did them any harm. I even used to flog the other members of staff. And I flogged dead horses! Why not? A bit more flogging would put the Great back in Britain . . .'

This went on twenty-four hours a day (Mrs Henslow even talked in her sleep). It was hardly surprising that she alone in the ward had no flowers or grapes. Nobody visited her. Nobody liked her.

One evening she got talking to Granny.

'This is a horrible place,' she said. 'I wouldn't come here if I wasn't ill. These nurses! Some of them are coloured, you know. Not that I'm a racist. But, well, the Nazis did have *some* good ideas . . .'

'I suppose so,' Granny agreed.

'This ward is so drab and uncomfortable.' Mrs Henslow leant towards Granny. 'Well, tomorrow I'm moving to a different hospital.'

'Are you?' Granny quavered.

'Oh, yes. You see, I have private medical insurance. Well, there was some sort of mix-up and it's taken them a few days to sort it out.

But tomorrow I'm off to a private hospital outside London. And I won't miss this place, I can tell you!'

'Lucky you,' Granny scowled. It had to be said that the ward wasn't the most comfortable of places.

'I am lucky. Tomorrow I'll have my own private room with a colour television and a nice view. The food there is absolutely delicious, I'm told. Brought in fresh from Harrods' Food Hall. You actually get a menu—not like here.'

Granny thought back to her lunch that day. It had been battered fish. It had been served underneath a battered tin dish. It hadn't been very hot. And it hadn't been very nice.

'I've heard this hospital is so nice,' Mrs Henslow went on, 'that people actually make themselves ill to get in there. My neighbour's wife cut off her hand to be admitted and she said it was worth every finger!' Mrs Henslow smiled. 'Of course I'm sure you'll get better *eventually* here. The NHS is wonderful really. If you're too poor to afford better.'

By now Granny was dark red with anger—and when the doctor came round later, it was discovered that her temperature had gone up to one hundred and five. Everyone assumed of course that it was her pneumonia that had caused the rise. The doctor doubted she would even live to see the next day and this is what he had reported to Mr and Mrs Warden who in turn had called in all the relatives.

But as it turned out, it was Mrs Henslow who suddenly took a turn for the worse during the night and quite unexpectedly died. Granny was lying awake—she was too angry to sleep—and actually heard the other lady breathe her last.

And that was what gave her the idea.

Granny had been perfectly content in the public ward until Mrs Henslow had described the hospital she was being transferred to. Food from Harrods? Colour TV and a view? Why couldn't she go there? Why *couldn't* she? Granny gazed at the still and silent figure in the next bed. By chance, Mrs Henslow was wearing a very similar nightie to her own. She was about the same age. And it was true, was it not, that one very old lady in bed with the sheets drawn up to her chin looks very much like the next. Mrs Henslow had no relatives or visitors to give the game away. The nurses and doctors had for the most part avoided her. Nobody had examined her that closely.

So why not?

Why not indeed?

And so it was that Granny swapped beds with Mrs Henslow and the following morning it was Mrs Henslow's death that was reported to Mr and Mrs Warden while Granny, her eyes peeping out over the sheet, was carried into a waiting ambulance and transferred to the private hospital.

And for the next few days—while Mrs Henslow was buried in the raging storm—it was Granny who reclined on duck down pillows watching her own 22-inch colour television whilst popping grapes, lychees and other exotic fruits between her lips. It didn't even matter when she forgot to answer to the name of Mrs Henslow. She was old. She was ill. She was bound to be confused.

Nobody noticed. It had all gone exactly according to plan.

*　　　*　　　*

There was an awkward silence at breakfast the next day. Mr and Mrs Warden hadn't slept a wink and it showed. Mr Warden had eaten his muesli dry and then poured half a pint of milk over his toast and marmalade. Mrs Warden had cleaned her teeth with her husband's shaving foam and was quite literally frothing at the mouth. For his part, Joe hadn't intended to come down to breakfast. But he was fed up being ill and wanted to get back to school—which meant he had to start eating.

'Jordan . . .' Mr Warden said.

Irma, who happened to be passing at that moment, dropped her tray and gasped. In all the years she had been with the Wardens, she had never heard Mr Warden address his son at the breakfast table.

'It seems we have matters to discuss,' Mr Warden went on. 'I suggest we meet this evening.'

'This morning!' Mrs Warden interrupted.

'I shall return early from work and we shall meet this afternoon,' Mr Warden decided. 'Half past four in the living-room. Irma will bake a cake. We shall have tea. As a family.'

'As a family!' Irma exclaimed. 'Are you feeling ill, Mr Warden, sir?'

'Yes. I am feeeling extremely ill as a matter of fact,' Mr Warden replied. 'But that is what we shall do.'

After breakfast, Mr Warden went to work. Mrs Warden went shopping. And Joe stayed at home. His thoughts were buzzing. He had seen the change in his parents. It was incredible. It was astounding. Could it be that . . .? Somehow, had they decided to believe him? Joe got dressed and went out feeling more alive than he had in weeks.

But neither Joe nor his parents had a particularly nice day.

'I'll come back . . .'

Mr Warden tried to concentrate on his work in his office but Granny's words echoed over and over in his head. Where would she pop up? Under his desk? In his filing cabinet? Outside the window . . . even if it was twenty-seven floors up? He reached for a cigar and rolled it against his cheek, taking in the aroma of the tobacco. 'You're being ridiculous,' he muttered to himself.

Somebody touched him lightly on the shoulder. Mr Warden screamed and jumped three feet into the air. The cigar slipped and disappeared into his left ear. Then he saw who it was. It was his secretary. She was looking at him in dismay.

'Lock the doors,' Mr Warden whimpered. 'Lock the filing cabinets. Lock everything! I want to be on my own . . .'

'I'll come back . . .'

Mrs Warden was at the Brent Cross shopping centre. There wasn't anything she particularly needed but she often found that buying things cheered her up. Once, when she was particularly depressed she had bought three lampshades, a deck chair, an umbrella and two pairs of gloves without actually wanting any of them. She was in that sort of mood. She was thinking of buying a Swiss Army knife. It might come in useful if she ever decided to join the Swiss Army.

She was standing on the escalator, travelling up past the central fountain, when she saw the figure standing at the top, waiting for her. She blinked. The yellow cheeks, the crooked smile, the gleaming eyes . . . it couldn't be! Mrs Warden stared. The escalator carried her ever nearer. It was!

'No!' she screamed. 'Go away, Mummy!

Turning round, Mrs Warden clambered down the up escalator, pushing the other shoppers out of the way. People were shouting at her, trying to stop her, but she ignored them. She just had to get back down. She could feel the metal beneath her feet carrying her the other way. It was like her worst nightmare come true. 'No!' she wailed again, shouldering her way past a pair of newly-weds and scattering parcels and packages everywhere. Then somehow her foot got tangled in the escalator, she dived forward, turned a somersault and landed spread-eagled on the marble floor.

'Is she all right?'

'I think she's had a fit.'

'She went mad!'

Security men were running towards her from every direction. With a soft moan, Mrs Warden looked back up the escalator. And there it was. What had frightened her wasn't Granny at all. It was a full-size cardboard cut-out of a dinosaur. It stood outside a video store with a sign reading 'FANTASIA— BUY IT HERE'. How could she possibly have made that mistake? Was she going mad?

The first security guard had reached her. Everyone was looking at her. Mrs Warden slowly began to laugh.

'I'll come back . . .'

Joe saw Granny everywhere. During the course of the day she had popped out of the fridge, out of the toaster, out of the dustbin and out of the fireplace. She had risen, dripping water, out of the pond and clawed her way up through the lawn. The clouds had twisted themselves into Granny's shape. The birds in the trees had winked at him with her eyes. Twice,

Irma had become Granny and even Wolfgang had momentarily borrowed her shadow.

It was all imagination, of course. The real horror was still to come.

That afternoon at four o'clock, Mr and Mrs Warden sat in the living-room with Joe and the tea that Irma had prepared. The Hungarian cook had decided that it was such an important occasion that she had gone quite mad. There were huge piles of sandwiches, home-made scones, sausage rolls, tea cakes, crumpets, cakes, biscuits and even a jelly. But no one was eating. Mrs Warden was a nervous wreck. Her hair was all over the place . . . and not only on her head. Mr Warden had bitten all his nails and was now starting on his wife's. Even Joe was trembling.

'I have called this meeting,' Mr Warden began, 'because I have something important to say.'

'Yes, that's right,' Mrs Warden agreed.

Then the telephone rang.

Mrs Warden sighed. 'I'll get it,' she said.

She stood up and walked across the room. The telephone was standing on a little antique table. She picked up the receiver. 'Hello? Maud N. Warden . . .' she said.

There was a moment's silence.

Then Mrs Warden let out a great scream and dropped the receiver as if it were a scorpion she had accidentally grasped. Everyone stared at her. Joe had never seen his mother like it. Her hair, already in disarray, was actually standing up on end, like in a cartoon. Her eyes were bulging. All the colour had drained out of her lips—including even the colour of her lipstick.

'It's her!' she screamed—but the sound came out as a hoarse, strangled whisper.

'That's nonsense!' Mr Warden muttered. 'I mean. Really, Maud. It's not possible.'

But Mrs Warden could only point at the telephone with a wobbling finger. 'It's her!' she groaned again.

'What did she say?' Mr Warden burbled.

'She said . . . she was coming back!'

'It's not possible.' Mr Warden strode forward and snatched up the receiver. 'Who is this?' he demanded.

Another pause. Joe waited silently. He hadn't breathed since the telephone rang.

Mr Warden's mouth fell open. Now he was holding the receiver away from him, as if it could suck him in down the wire. 'No!' he shouted at it. 'Go away! We don't want you!' And with that he hung up—so hard that he actually broke the telephone into several pieces.

'It was her!' Mrs Warden whimpered.

'It was her,' Mr Warden agreed. 'I'd know that voice anywhere.'

'What did she say?' Joe asked.

'She said she was much better now and she'd be here in half an hour.'

'Much better?' Joe shuddered. 'How can you be much better when you're dead?' Somewhere in the back of his mind he knew that the whole thing was ridiculous. Ghosts didn't announce their arrival by telephone. But seeing his parents as terrified as they were he decided to go along with them. It was better than being left on his own.

'Half an hour . . .' Mrs Warden whispered. And that was when the full horror of it hit her. 'Half an hour!' she screamed.

'Pack!' Mr Warden yelled.

Exactly twenty-nine minutes later, the front door of Thattlebee Hall burst open and the Wardens tumbled out grasping two hastily packed suitcases. Mrs Warden had thrown on her favourite fur coat. Mr Warden was clutching his wallet, the family passports and his eighteen favourite credit cards. His car—a green Mercedes—was waiting for them at the front.

'In!' Mr Warden yelled, wrenching open the door and catching his wife with it on the head.

'Aaagh!' Mrs Warden cried.

'And me!' Joe shouted, piling into the back. He was actually enjoying all this.

'Quickly!' Mr Warden stabbed forward with the ignition key, missed and tried again. This time it went in.

He twisted and the Mercedes coughed into life.

At the same time, a taxi appeared, rumbling up the drive.

'There!'

'No!'

'Aaagh!'

'Mummy!'

'Help!'

Granny—the ghost of Granny—was in the back seat. There could be no mistaking her, sitting there, gazing out of the window—back from the dead! And this wasn't a dream. The entire family was seeing her at the same time.

Mr Warden wrenched the gear-stick and slammed his foot down on the accelerator. The car leapt forward.

Granny, sitting in the back of the taxi, frowned and pursed her lips. She had been released, fully recovered, from the hospital just half an hour before. She had of course telephoned to say she was coming and had been quite unable to understand the hysterical reactions of her daughter and son-in-law. And where were they going now? One moment the Mercedes was tearing down the drive, heading straight for the taxi. Then it had swerved to one side, ploughed across the lawn and then burst through a hedge onto the main road.

The taxi stopped and she got out.

'That'll be eighteen quid, love,' the taxi driver said.

With a snarl Granny slammed the car door behind her, breaking both the window and the taxi driver's nose. She strode across the lawn, her hands on her hips, and gazed at the hole in the hedge. They had gone. Left her. How could they?

Granny fell to her knees, lifted her hands to the sky and howled.

The storm broke a few minutes later.

EPILOGUE:
ANTHONY LAGOON

Anthony Lagoon was a cattle station in the middle of the Northern Territory of Australia. It consisted of a long, low wooden house with glass windows and a verandah which was the manager's house and four shacks for the workers. There was a water tower, a flaking metal cattle run and an airstrip. The nearest town, Mount Isa, was a two hour flight away. Nobody knew who Anthony was. But then the outback is full of people who prefer not to be remembered.

Mr Warden had bought Anthony Lagoon as soon as he had landed in Perth. He had seen it advertised for sale in the *Perth Exchange* and had made an instant decision.

'We'll be safe there,' he said. 'No roads. No telephones. No letters. She'll never find us.'

And six days later, after driving all

the way across Australia to Townsville, around the one-way system and then west again, they arrived.

There were four jackeroos working on Anthony Lagoon—all of them men on the run. Rolf had poisoned his wife. Barry and Bruce were wanted for armed robbery. And Les had been hiding for so long that he'd forgotten what it was he'd actually done although, as he frequently told the others, it must have been something brutal. These were tough, brutal men. Rolf had only one leg. He'd lost the other in a car accident and hadn't even noticed for a month. Bruce chewed live bullets and Barry scoured saucepans with his beard. Les could rip a cow in half with his bare hands. They were four of the ugliest, most violent men you could hope to meet. They only had one string vest between them and played poker to decide who would wear it.

You'd think Rolf, Barry, Bruce and Les would have made mincemeat out of the new owners of Anthony Lagoon but the surprising fact is that they quickly warmed to them. But then the Wardens had changed beyond all recognition.

Mr Warden had taken off his business suit and put on a pair of jeans, a brightly coloured shirt and a ten-gallon hat that came down to his nose. After only a week he had acquired an Australian accent. Having been stuck in an office all his life, he now found he loved the fresh air. Although there were over one hundred thousand head of cattle on the station, he had decided to get to know each and every one of them by name.

After all her riding lessons, Mrs Warden quickly impressed the jackeroos with her excellent horse riding. They decided they liked her as soon as she had galloped twice round the paddock blindfold and backwards. Then she set to work rebuilding the compound, repairing the fences, planting a garden, putting pretty lace curtains into Bruce and Barry's bedrooms and generally making the place more like home.

Mrs Warden also taught Joe how to

ride (she never called him Jordan now). Following her example, the four jackeroos decided to lend a hand with Joe's education and soon Joe knew everything there was to know about managing cattle and, for that matter, robbing banks.

Joe loved his life on the cattle station. He had so often dreamed of running away—to a circus, to the Foreign Legion, to wherever—that it took him a long time to realize that this was what he had actually done . . . even if his parents had rather surprised him by coming along too. But now every day was an adventure as he galloped across the paddocks under the hot Australian sun, dodging down to avoid the tree-spiders and surging, waist-deep, through the lagoons.

It was hard work. The day started at five when Joe rode out alone to get the horses in. Joe had never seen the dawn before and he marvelled at the thousand shades of red that shimmered over the horizon as the sun climbed up into the sky. He loved the smell of the air and the great silence of the plains and rapidly forgot Latin, Greek, Algebra, Geography and just about everything else he had been learning at school. Joe worked all day until sunset. There was no television on the station but he didn't miss it. He actually went to bed tired, not because he had to. And every ache, every pain, every cut and every blister was precious to him because it was part of the adventure.

Naturally, Joe lost weight. He grew tall and muscular with broad, suntanned shoulders. Once a month, Rolf, Barry, Bruce and Les took him with them to Mount Isa and he would stay up late into the night, drinking and gambling. That was the best thing. He was an equal. Nobody treated him like a child any more.

News has a strange way of travelling in Australia, crossing huge distances without the help of a stamp or a telephone line. And the happiness of the Wardens was completed one day by the arrival of someone who had heard they were there and had decided to join them. As soon as he saw who it was, Joe understood everything: the strange figure he had seen at Paddington Station, the last-minute rescue at the hotel and the anonymous postcard.

The new arrival was Mrs Jinks.

'I thought I was doomed when the police dogs came after me,' she explained, 'and indeed I was bitten quite badly. But I was very lucky. Just as I burst through the bushes, a large rabbit appeared. The dogs decided they preferred the taste of rabbit to me and attacked that instead. I managed to climb a tree and waited there until everyone had gone.'

'But you kept your eye on me after that, didn't you, Mrs Jinks?' Joe said.

'Well, yes. I couldn't reveal myself, unfortunately—I was still wanted for theft, after all. But I was frightened to leave you on your own and when your granny came to look after you I knew something was going on. I followed you to Bideford in disguise and I was there at the Stilton International when they tied you to that horrible device.'

'And it was you in the dark.' Joe shivered. 'It was lucky the lights fused.'

'That wasn't luck at all. That was me. I turned the power off at the main fuse box and then crept onto the stage to untie you.'

'I got your card,' Joe said.

'Yes. I thought it was time your parents knew the truth. Of course, I couldn't tell them myself. So I hoped a little nudge would do the trick.'

Mr and Mrs Warden were delighted to see Mrs Jinks. They knew now that they had been deceived and couldn't apologize enough. They immediately invited her to stay with them at the cattle station and Joe was delighted when she agreed.

And so time passed at Anthony Lagoon which was a very pretty place now with a duck pond, a village green, two English sheepdogs, a willow tree and a beautiful croquet lawn. Often, when the day's work was done, Mrs Jinks would stroll out with Joe and they would talk about what had happened.

'Do you think she'll ever find us?' Joe asked one evening.

'Who, dearest?'

'Granny. The ghost of Granny.'

Mrs Jinks looked past the verandah where Mr Warden was pushing Mrs Warden on a swing and beyond over the outback to the deep red glow where the setting sun marked the end of the world. 'No,' she said. 'I don't think so.'

'I hated her.' Joe shuddered. 'Old people are horrible.'

'No,' Mrs Jinks corrected him. 'There's nothing wrong with being old. Don't forget—you'll be old one day. Nobody can avoid it.'

'Well, I won't be like Granny,' Joe said.

'Of course you won't,' Mrs Jinks agreed. 'If you're kind and cheerful when you're young, you'll be kind and cheerful when you're old . . . only more so. Old age is like a magnifying glass. It takes the best and the worst of you and magnifies them. Granny was selfish and cruel all her life. But you can't blame her for being old.'

'She could still find us here.' Joe's eyes—older and more knowing—scanned the horizon. He shivered in the cool evening breeze.

192

'It doesn't matter any more,' Mrs Jinks replied. 'Even if she did find you . . . you're ready for her now.'

*   *   *

In fact Granny died two years later—this time for real. After the Wardens had left she had found there was nobody to look after her and had rapidly gone into a decline. This was her tragedy. All the spitefulness of her life had caught up with her and suddenly she was alone.

Her hair had never grown again after the accident and although she had been given new false teeth, they didn't fit, with the result that she couldn't talk or eat solids. She was moved to an Old People's Home next to a cement factory and spent the next two years on her own, sipping porridge through a straw. In an attempt to cheer her up, the matron of the home gave her a parrot. The parrot bit her. The wound went septic. And that was what finally finished her off.

That was a year ago.

But Granny is not forgotten. Deep in the heart of the Australian outback, the aborigines gather around a huge camp fire. Their black bodies are painted and they sit quite naked apart from a twist of cloth around their loins. Then the music of the didgeridoo throbs and wails through the darkness and if the magic is working a figure appears, wrapped in a thick coat against the desert chill. The aborigines see her scowling in the light of the fire, her eyes glowing, her mouth opening and closing as she chews on her invisible feast. They call her 'old-woman-walk-by-night'.

It is Granny. Looking for Joe.

But she hasn't found him yet.